Saying good-bye . . .

Mr. Stewart glanced at his watch. "Honey, I've got to go," he said hoarsely.

Molly couldn't speak.

"You know I'll always be thinking of you, always missing you," he said. "But I'll be back before you know it."

Swallowing hard, Molly forced herself to nod.

Her father came over and sat on the window seat. Taking her hands in his, he said, "You know, honey, by staying here at Glenmore you're helping make my dream come true. I've been dreaming of this movie for the last five years, and finally I have a chance to make it. Thank you for understanding."

Looking into her father's brown eyes, Molly felt a renewed determination to be brave for his sake. He was the most important person in the world to her, and she knew that she was to him, too. "Oh, Dad, I love you so much," she whispered.

Then he was hugging her tightly, so tightly her ribs began to ache, but she held on to him with all her might. This was good-bye.

Don't miss the other books in this
heartwarming new series:

Princess

#2: *A Room in the Attic*

#3: *Home at Last*

Princess

BOOK 1

Molly's Heart

GABRIELLE CHARBONNET

AN
APPLE
PAPERBACK

SCHOLASTIC INC.
New York Toronto London Auckland Sydney

ISBN 0-590-22287-2

Copyright © 1995 by Daniel Weiss Associates, Inc., and Gabrielle C. Varela. All rights reserved. Published by Scholastic Inc. APPLE PAPERBACKS ® is a registered trademark of Scholastic Inc.

Produced by Daniel Weiss Associates, Inc.
33 West 17th Street, New York, NY 10011

12 11 10 9 8 7 6 5 4 3 2   5 6 7 8 9/9 0/0

Printed in the U.S.A.   40

First Scholastic printing, May 1995

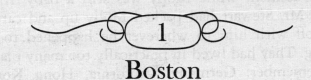

1

Boston

At the end of the wooden pier, the sun beat down upon the waves so brightly that Molly squinted.

I want to stay here, she thought, swallowing hard. *I want to stay here forever, just me and Dad.* Her bare toes curled against the rough, splintery wood of the pier. A breeze, with all the summer's heat burned out of it, brushed through her long, straight blond hair.

It wasn't even September yet, but already summer had left the island of Nantucket. And now Molly was leaving, too.

"There you are, sweetie—I've been looking for you." Molly's father, Michael Stewart, walked down the pier toward his ten-year-old daughter. Like her, he had straight blond hair, but his was lighter, almost golden, and cut short. His eyes were a warm brown, while hers were green.

Molly felt his hand on her shoulder.

"Are you saying good-bye?" he asked gently.

Molly nodded. She and her father had lived all

1

over the world together. Molly's mother had died in a car accident while Molly was still a baby. After that, Mr. Stewart had packed Molly up and carted her off with him to wherever he happened to be going. They had lived in practically too many places to remember: Germany, California, Hong Kong, Tokyo, New York—wherever her father was making his movies.

When Molly was little, she and her father had started the tradition of saying good-bye to whatever place they were leaving. They would stand in a favorite spot and memorize the view; then they would tell it good-bye, and promise to return one day.

Molly took her father's hand and stared out at Nantucket Bay. The chilly, olive-green waves were cresting playfully, the sun shone with a gentle warmth, the seagulls wheeled and circled overhead. All summer she had walked on this beach, swum in this water, fished off this pier. Ahead of her, to the northeast, was Boston, Massachusetts. By dinnertime that night she and her father would be there.

"Good-bye, Nantucket," Mr. Stewart said, looking out at the waves. "I promise we'll be back."

Molly swallowed hard again. "Good-bye, Nantucket," she repeated, forcing her voice not to waver. "I promise we'll be back." Her father squeezed her hand.

Twenty minutes later their rented summer house was closed up, forlorn and empty, the shady porch swept clean of sand. As she and her father drove away down the winding, pretty country road, Molly refused to look back.

"Would the young lady like a hamburger, perhaps? We have a lovely steak we could chop up for you." The waiter, dressed in a formal black coat, spoke to Molly as if she were five years old. Outside the window of the restaurant, the lights of Boston shone like fireflies. Molly and her father had checked into Brown's Hotel, which was one of the most exclusive and expensive hotels in Boston. They had stayed there before, almost two years earlier.

Across the table, Molly's father let his eyes twinkle at her.

Molly smiled at her father. He knew how she hated being talked down to. She spoke to the waiter politely. "No, thank you. The young lady would like to start with the littleneck clams on the half shell, and then I think the filet mignon, cooked medium-rare. Also, I'll have the spinach soufflé on the side, and we need more mineral water, please." She daintily took a sip from her water glass, then dabbed her lips with her napkin.

The waiter looked shocked, but he nodded respectfully. After Mr. Stewart had ordered and the waiter had scuttled away, Molly and her father shared a quiet laugh.

Her father took her hand across the table and

held it. "Oh, sweetie, I'm going to miss you so much."

Instantly Molly's smile faded. He had mentioned the one thing she was trying so hard not to think about.

"I'm going to miss you, too," she said, feeling a lump come into her throat for the second time that day. "Dad, are you positive I can't come with you? I've always come with you before." She'd asked that question during the summer, but she had to ask it one last time.

Her father looked sad. "Yes, sweetie, I'm sure. The Brazilian rain forest is going to be hard enough for me and the film crew—it'd be impossible to have you there, too. The place we're filming is really a pain to get to, and what would we do about school?" He squeezed her hand. The waiter came and put a small basket of hot rolls on their table.

When they were alone again, Mr. Stewart continued. "The film I want to make might take more than a year, and it's going to be very difficult. I can't even take my usual crew. Only a small group of tough professionals will be going with me."

He took a sip of his drink. "No, I'm sure we're doing the right thing by enrolling you at Glenmore. It's one of the best boarding schools in the country. I'll be able to really concentrate on the movie, knowing that you're safe and surrounded by new friends in a good school. Plus, you'll love Boston.

4

It's a pretty town." He waved a piece of roll at her. "When I come back, you can show me around."

Molly nodded stiffly. So she wouldn't have to speak, she took a bite of a roll herself. After a minute she said in a low voice, "It's just that we've never been apart before, Dad."

"I know, princess. Believe me, it's going to be just as hard on me as it is on you. I don't know what I'll do without my best little traveler and number-one assistant." He smiled at her fondly. "But we had a great summer, didn't we?"

"Yeah, we did," Molly answered, forcing herself to smile. "It was wonderful."

Then a thought occurred to her, one she had pushed away many times before. "Dad, will it be dangerous for you where you're going?"

"No, no, of course not. The government wants me to be there, and I'm sure they'll take good care of me." Mr. Stewart was going to make a documentary about the struggle between the environmentalists and the native Brazilian people. He was hoping his film would call attention to the difficult situation in the rain forest. "Don't worry, *chou-chou*," he continued. "I'll call and write as much as I can."

Chou-chou was a nickname that Molly had had in France. Basically it meant "little cabbage." But it was a good nickname, not a mean one.

Molly speared a littleneck clam with her fork and popped it into her mouth. "Okay. I'll try not to

5

worry." But inside, she knew she would worry every minute they were apart.

"Oh, Dad," Molly said, laughing so hard she could hardly speak. "Stop it, stop it!"

Her father grinned at her from behind an enormous stuffed elephant. Once more he raised his hand in front of his face as though it were a trunk, and he trumpeted. People in the huge toy store turned to stare.

Giggling, Molly ducked behind a large display of computer games. "I don't know you," she informed her father in a loud whisper. "You're a total stranger, and we're not related."

Laughing, her father swooped out from behind the elephant and grabbed Molly in a tight hug.

"No such luck," he said cheerfully. "You look just like your old dad."

Across from them was a mirrored column. Arm in arm, they smiled into it. They did look alike, mostly in their coloring. But Molly's green eyes, her small, straight nose, her wide mouth: those were all her mother's.

Mr. Stewart checked his watch. "Okay. Let's look at our schedule. Almost time for afternoon tea at the Prince George."

Molly gasped with pleasure. "Oh, Dad, really?" She loved going to fancy places for tea. When they had been in London making Mr. Stewart's film

Castle for Hire, they had gone as often as possible.

"Yes, really. But first I think we need some more toys. I'm going to be gone for a while, so you'll need lots of stuff to keep you busy."

Molly's mood deflated a little when he mentioned his leaving. It was getting closer all the time, like a disaster she couldn't prevent. Shaking her head, she decided not to think about it. "Dad, I don't need any more stuff."

But her father was already at the rack of interactive computer games. "Do you have this one?" He held up a cartridge, and she nodded. "How about this one?" When Molly shook her head, he put it into the large basket on his arm. It was already stuffed full of pretty stationery sets ("to write your old dad on"), arts and crafts materials, board games, card games, a huge watercolor pen set, and a medium-sized stuffed polar bear. Four other baskets, equally full, were already parked by the checkout counter, waiting for them.

Molly sighed patiently as her father went through the rack of computer games. This was like Christmas and her birthday—no, like *two* Christmases and *three* birthdays—all rolled into one. She knew her father had lots of money; after all, he'd directed or produced some of the biggest, most successful movies of the past ten years. And wherever they had been, all over the world, they had always lived in fabulous houses or apartments or hotels. But

Molly knew this shopping spree was just because he felt sad about leaving.

Ever since she was a baby, it had been just the two of them, wherever they were. The longest they had ever been apart was when she had gone on sleepovers at a friend's house. But now her father was going away without her, and he would be gone more than a year. Her mind swirled with dismay, and numbly she followed her dad to the checkout register at the front of the store.

Molly was so full she felt like lying down in the middle of the sidewalk with her arms out to her sides. That hot-fudge sundae had definitely been a mistake, especially after the milk shake and the huge piece of apple pie.

"Can we sit down for a minute?" she asked, heading toward a green-painted bench nearby.

Mr. Stewart nodded, pulling a small street map out of his jacket pocket. Molly sat down, leaned back, and closed her eyes. For the last five days, they had done just about everything there was to do in Boston. They had gone to movies, to a modern play that Molly had hated, to art museums . . . but most of all, they had shopped.

Molly's last school had been the American School in Taipei, Taiwan, and she had worn a uniform there. But at Glenmore she would wear her own clothes, and her father had insisted that she get a whole new wardrobe. Not only had she grown out of a lot of her clothes, but her father said he wanted her to "wow the other students."

"I thought no one was supposed to know that my dad's a famous movie producer," Molly had countered.

"Well, yeah," her father had agreed. "Don't you think it'll be better if the other kids like you because you're you, instead of sucking up to you because they want to be the next Macauley Culkin?"

"And nine pairs of corduroys from Ralph Lauren will make them like me for me?" she had asked, rolling her eyes.

"No," her father had said mischievously. "But you're forgetting the six pairs of loafers from Gucci."

Now she felt all shopped out. Sitting there on the bench in the mild, almost-autumn weather was really nice—as long as she didn't think about what would happen the day after tomorrow.

"Are we going back to the hotel now?" she mumbled tiredly.

"Uh-uh. We have one more stop to make today. Don't worry, it isn't far from here."

Groaning, Molly let her father pull her to her feet, and she plodded after him down the sidewalk. Soon they stopped in front of a huge, run-down-looking building.

"What is this place?" Molly asked.

"It's the Boston Garden," Mr. Stewart said proudly. "There's a cat show going on." He beamed down at her.

Molly stared at him. "A cat show?" Had her father lost his mind?

Two hours later, in the backseat of their limo, Molly clutched a small wicker basket on her lap. Every now and then a tiny, blue-velvet paw darted through the grate and swiped at Molly's lap. Molly giggled.

She held the basket up and looked inside. A small, intensely fuzzy kitten with downy, blue-gray fur stared back at her.

"Hi there, Mr. Tibbs," Molly said gently. "You're so cute. You're coming to live with me. I can't wait to play with you." She looked up at her father. "Are you sure they allow pets at Glenmore?" she asked suspiciously.

Her father looked determined. "Let's just say that they'll allow *this* pet for *you*," he said.

Molly leaned back against the seat. Mr. Tibbs swiped at her again, pushing against the grate of his carrier. Molly grinned at him. "Anyway, he's totally adorable—I love him. Thanks, Dad."

Her father smiled down at her. "Anything you want, princess," he said fondly. "You know that." He leaned back with his arm around her.

Holding Mr. Tibbs's basket against her, Molly thought, *Anything but the one thing I want. Which is to be with you.*

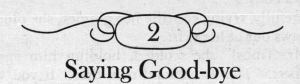

2

Saying Good-bye

Molly twirled slowly in front of the full-length mirror in her room at Brown's Hotel. Her father was waiting for her in the living room of their suite. It was their absolute last night together before she went to Glenmore. She wanted to look her best.

The dress was a new one. It had a green velvet top and a plaid taffeta pouf skirt. She wore dark-green tights and black velvet flats. Her long blond hair was pulled away from her face and clasped with a green velvet bow.

In the mirror she saw a thin girl with large green eyes, tall for her age, with a tiny bit of summer tan left. *No matter what, I'm not going to cry tonight,* she told herself fiercely. *It would just make Dad feel much worse. I'm going to be brave.*

"Yaaghh!" she screamed as Mr. Tibbs launched himself from the edge of the bed at her. His small, fuzzy body hit her skirt, and instantly all his claws

11

were out as he began to climb determinedly up Molly's body.

Carefully, trying to stifle her giggles, she plucked his claws out of her skirt.

"Mr. Tibbs!" she scolded, holding him against her chest. "This is a brand-new dress! If you want me to hold you, just say so. Don't *fling* yourself at me." The small kitten rubbed his head against her chin, and he began purring. Molly stroked him softly.

"Oh, Tibbsey," she sighed. "After tomorrow you're going to be my best friend—my only friend. Will you help me be not so lonely at Glenmore? Will you cheer me up?"

As if in response, Mr. Tibbs patted her chin with his soft paw.

Mr. Stewart tapped on the door. "Mols? You ready, honey?"

Feeling a tiny bit better, Molly set Mr. Tibbs down on the bed. "We won't be long, Tibbsey," she promised. "Guard the room." With a last smile at her kitten, she went to meet her father.

Two hours later, Molly pushed away her dessert plate with a satisfied sigh. "That was the best cheesecake I've ever had," she announced.

Her father smiled at her. "Better than the cheese-cake we had at Empress of the Nile in Cairo, when we were making *Mummy's Day Out*?"

Molly thought about it. "Yes. Definitely better."

Her father suddenly looked serious. He took a small velvet box out of his jacket pocket. "This belonged to your mother," Mr. Stewart said, pushing it across the table. "I always kept it to remember her by. Now I want you to have it to remember *me* by."

Feeling tears starting to burn at the corners of her eyes, Molly said, "I don't need anything to remember you by—you're part of me."

"Open it," he said softly.

Gulping, Molly opened the little box.

"Oh!" she gasped. Inside was a small gold locket in the shape of a heart. Engraved on one side were her father's initials, MPS, for Michael Patrick Stewart. On the other side was MDS, for Marielle Duvalier Stewart. Molly's mother had been French. Carefully Molly pressed the minuscule latch and the locket opened. A tiny black and white picture of her mother was on the left. She looked young and beautiful, and she was smiling at the camera. Facing that picture on the other side was a tiny picture of Molly's father. He, too, looked young and happy and carefree.

Molly glanced up to see a look of terrible sadness on her father's face. That did it. She threw down her linen napkin, dropped her head into her hands, and burst into tears.

The next day was gray and drizzly, with a slight chill in the air. Molly thought the weather suited

13

her mood perfectly. The world was weeping along with her.

At two o'clock in the afternoon she and her father drove up to Glenmore in their limousine. The chauffeur pulled to a stop at the curb. Molly leaned against the window and looked out at the building that was to be her home for the next year.

Glenmore was on a pretty street in the Back Bay area of Boston. Four blocks of old, impressive townhouses bordered a private park in the middle, which was called Fitzgerald Square. Glenmore took up almost a whole block by itself. The main building was large, four stories high, with big windows and carved gargoyles on the roof. To the left, very close to the school, was a townhouse. Molly didn't know if it was part of Glenmore or not. Some of the buildings around the square were now apartments, and some had offices on their first floors.

In the car, Mr. Stewart took her hand. "Ready to face the natives?" he asked with a smile. He always said that when they arrived in a new place.

Molly nodded, still looking at all the buildings. "Ready as I'll ever be."

The chauffeur jumped out to open their doors, and Molly climbed out, carrying Mr. Tibbs's wicker basket. He mewed softly. Molly looked up at Glenmore from the sidewalk. She could see a few curtains twitching back as students checked her out. She already felt lonely.

14

There were stone steps leading up to the large, dark wooden doors. Before Molly and Mr. Stewart got to the top step, the door was opened by a small, pretty woman wearing a stylish business suit. She had dark, wavy hair cut in a chin-length bob, fair skin, and dark eyes. She looked friendly and professional.

"Hello!" she said with a big smile. "Welcome to Glenmore. I'm Cathy Thacker, the headmistress." She laughed. "*Headmistress* sounds so old-fashioned, doesn't it? But my husband and I run Glenmore. You must be Molly Stewart, and Mr. Stewart." She smiled again and stretched out her hand to shake his. "I'd like to take this opportunity, Mr. Stewart, to tell you how very much I've enjoyed your films."

Mr. Stewart squeezed Molly's hand. "Thanks," he said.

Then Ms. Thacker stood back and cheerfully motioned for them to enter Glenmore.

Molly hadn't been sure what to expect, but now she saw that the inside of the main building looked like a cross between a regular school and a house. They were standing in a large lobby, with patterned carpet on the floor and old-fashioned oil paintings hanging on the walls.

A wooden counter stood against one wall, and a young woman sat there, looking at them in a friendly way. A telephone rang and she answered it, saying, "Glenmore," in a soft voice.

15

There were three sets of double wooden doors that Molly could see, and they were pointed at the top, like a church's doors. Molly could hear the sounds of kids talking and laughing and yelling, and upstairs it sounded as if someone was dragging a suitcase down a hall.

If this had been a hotel where she and her father were going to settle down for several months while he worked on a movie, Molly would have enjoyed looking around. But knowing that at this time tomorrow she would be here alone, and her father would be far, far away in the Brazilian rain forest, made her feel desperately sad.

Just then another, smaller door opened, and a man came out.

Ms. Thacker turned to him and said, "Jerry, this is Mr. Stewart and his daughter, Molly. Mr. Stewart, this is my husband, Jerry Thacker. His grandfather founded Glenmore."

Molly's father shook his hand as Molly studied Mr. Thacker. In the last year or so, she had been thinking that she might want to be a writer when she grew up. Mr. Stewart had a friend who worked for a newspaper, and he always made the job sound like fun. So Molly had been keeping a journal and trying to notice everything around her as much as possible. You never knew when you might need a detail for a story, she figured.

Now she looked at the Thackers and wondered

what they were like. They both seemed pretty nice. Ms. Thacker seemed more outgoing and friendly than her husband. He seemed quieter and plainer somehow.

"Dear," Ms. Thacker said to Molly, "why don't we get you settled in your room first, and then your father and I can discuss some details in the office. Will you come with me?" She led the way through the double doors at the end of the large foyer, and then down another hall to the left. At the end of the hall were double glass doors, and they went through those, too. Mr. Tibbs's basket was beginning to feel very heavy.

"This is Camden Hall," Ms. Thacker told them. "On the first floor are the administrative offices, the kitchen and dining room, and the nurse's station. Upstairs is the girls' dorm."

They stopped in front of two elevators with fancy wooden doors. When the elevator came, Ms. Thacker pushed the button for three. "You're on the third floor, dear," she told Molly. "There are stairs opposite the elevators, and we encourage the students to exercise their legs as much as possible." She gave a little laugh.

When the elevator doors opened, two girls were waiting for it. They had been talking and laughing, but stopped respectfully when they saw Ms. Thacker.

"Ah, Rebecca and Davina," Ms. Thacker said.

17

"Please meet your new schoolmate, Molly Stewart. Molly, dear, this is Rebecca Hirschman and Davina Etheridge. Rebecca is in sixth grade, and Davina is in seventh."

The two girls stepped forward and formally offered their hands for shaking.

"Hi," Rebecca said, pumping Molly's hand.

"Hello," said Davina. She had an English accent. Both girls wore wide smiles. Molly couldn't tell if they were actually friendly or if they were just acting that way in front of Ms. Thacker. For the moment she gave them the benefit of the doubt.

"Run along, girls," Ms. Thacker said. "Follow me, Molly. Your room is here on the main hall. I know it seems confusing right now, but Glenmore isn't actually all that big. I'm sure you'll know your way around in no time." Ms. Thacker gave Molly a reassuring smile as she walked down the third-floor corridor and stopped in front of a wide, white-painted door.

"For now you can acquaint yourself with your own room. Our girls usually share their rooms, but your father requested that you have your privacy. So here we are." With a small flourish, Ms. Thacker flung open the door to a large, comfortably furnished bedroom.

Not bad, Molly thought. She was glad she wouldn't have to share her room with anyone—except Mr. Tibbs, of course. Setting down his wicker carrier, Molly walked into the room that would be her home for the next year.

It was about as big as a nice hotel room, she decided as she looked around. There were two large windows that looked out over the street. Through them she could see Fitzgerald Square. The windows had window seats with cushions on them, which was pretty cool. Her twin-size bed was made of white-painted iron all in curlicues. The walls were covered with flowered wallpaper. All in all, it was a little too fancy for her taste, but better than she'd expected. Best of all, she had her own bathroom, and a large closet. There was an alcove next to the bathroom that had a small love seat, an armchair, and a desk with a chair.

"Now, Molly, why don't you get settled in a bit?" Ms. Thacker said. "Marcus will be up in a minute with your luggage and your trunk. Your daddy and I will be downstairs in my office."

Mr. Stewart came over to where Molly was looking out of one window. "Okay, sweetie?" he asked in a low voice.

Molly turned and nodded at him, trying to look calm and brave. "Sure. I'll see you in a while."

Ms. Thacker and Molly's father left, and soon a large, heavily built man wheeled her suitcases in on a little cart. He made a second trip for her trunk.

For a few moments after Marcus left, Molly sat on a window seat and gazed at her luggage. She always enjoyed unpacking in a new place—whether it was a rented apartment in London or New York, a hotel in Spain, or even a hut on the Philippine coast. Whenever she and her father arrived at a new movie location, she always unpacked right away, putting things in drawers and closets, making it seem more like home—even if it was just a trailer home in the back lot of a movie studio.

But this was different. This really was going to be her home for the next year. And her father would be gone. It would be just Molly and 120 other students, only two of whom she had met so far.

An annoyed *mew!* broke into Molly's thoughts, and a small blue paw swiped angrily outside the wicker basket.

"Oh, Mr. Tibbs!" Molly cried, rushing over to him. "I'm sorry. I completely forgot. *You'd* better get used to our new home, too." She unlatched the basket, and instantly Mr. Tibbs tumbled out, an indignant ball of blue-gray fluff. After giving Molly a reproachful glance with his baby-blue eyes, he immediately stalked off into his new surroundings, his small tail standing up like an exclamation point.

Grinning, Molly scrambled through her bags and boxes and found her pet supplies. The first thing she did was set up Mr. Tibbs's litter box in her white marble bathroom. Then she fixed his own little bed in the corner, next to her bed. She knew he would probably just sleep with her, but the small four-poster cat bed had been so funny she and her dad hadn't been able to resist it.

The next time she looked up, Mr. Tibbs was sitting importantly on a window seat, washing his face. She smiled, her first real smile of the day. Then she began to unpack.

The late-afternoon sun shone down on Fitzgerald Square. Molly, standing at her window, fingered the gold locket around her neck.

"The room's okay, honey?" her father asked. "I wanted a suite, but they didn't have any." He frowned. "I could have them knock down a wall."

Molly turned to smile at him, a forced, wavering smile. "Don't be silly, Dad. It's fine."

"And you met some of the other kids this afternoon?"

"Yeah. There was an orientation for everyone, boys and girls." Molly wrinkled her nose. "Some of them seem stuck-up, especially the eighth-graders. They think they run the place." Glenmore was only a middle school: the students there were in sixth, seventh, or eighth grade. Molly was at the bottom of the list, a freshman sixth-grader. Because she would be eleven in December, they had let her skip into sixth grade. Otherwise she would have had to go to another school.

Her father frowned. "Well, if anyone gives you any trouble, just kick their butt."

21

Molly couldn't help giggling at the thought of her Gucci loafers making an imprint on someone's designer backside.

Mr. Stewart glanced at his watch. "Honey, I've got to go," he said hoarsely.

Molly couldn't speak.

"The mail system in the rain forest is very primitive, to say the least," he said. "But I'll try to get my hands on a cellular phone. You know I'll always be thinking of you, always missing you. But I'll be back before you know it."

Swallowing hard, Molly forced herself to nod.

Her father came over and sat on the window seat. Taking her hands in his, he said, "You know, honey, by staying here at Glenmore you're helping make my dream come true. I know I can make a special film about the rain forest—a film that will open people's eyes, maybe even change things. I've been dreaming of this movie for the last five years, and finally I have a chance to make it. Thank you for understanding."

Looking into her father's brown eyes, Molly felt a renewed determination to be brave for his sake. He was the most important person in the world to her, and she knew that she was to him, too. "Oh, Dad, I love you so much," she whispered.

Then he was hugging her tightly, so tightly her ribs began to ache, but she held on to him with all her might. This was good-bye.

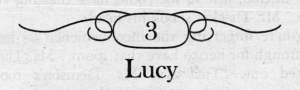

3

Lucy

In her office, Cathy Thacker stacked some completed forms neatly on her desk. She glanced at the clock. Almost nine o'clock. The door that connected her office with her husband's opened, and Jerry poked his timid face in.

"Don't hover, Jerry," Ms. Thacker said mildly. "Come in and shut the door."

"So, ready for our first day?" he asked, pacing up and down, rubbing his hands.

Ms. Thacker sighed. "I guess so." She frowned at a stack of school records. "I have no idea why people can't seem to fill these things in properly. The instructions seem perfectly clear to me."

"How's the Stewart girl doing?" Mr. Thacker asked.

Ms. Thacker grinned. "Our new star pupil? She seems okay. Missing her indulgent father already. We'll have to make sure she's happy here, and that she isn't too lonely."

23

"I still can't believe Stewart paid double our usual tuition, just so she could have that big single room." Mr. Thacker shook his head.

"You're forgetting the inconvenience *we* had to go through for her to have that room," Ms. Thacker pointed out. "That was Ms. Denison's room— remember, we had to move the dorm mother to another floor. *And* he's paying extra so that she can have a pet and a TV in her room."

"Right, right," her husband said, nodding. "That's true. All the same, he didn't even bat an eye. Just wrote out the check." Mr. Thacker smiled. "A few more students like her and we'd be doing okay, huh?"

Ms. Thacker smiled back. "We'd be doing more than okay."

Knock knock.

Molly wiped her eyes and looked at her door. It was almost nine o'clock, when classes would start. She knew she should go down—she had already missed breakfast—but she hated for the other kids to see her with watery eyes and a red nose. Now someone had come to get her.

"It's open," Molly finally called.

The door opened, and a girl maybe a little older than Molly walked in. She was shorter than Molly, and plump. Her brown hair was cut in a chin-length bob, which made her face seem even rounder. Wire-rimmed glasses perched on her nose.

24

"Hi," she said in a friendly voice. "You're a new girl. Well, of course. I'm Lucy. Lucy Axminster. I'm an old girl. They sent me up to get you. All the new girls get an old girl to help show them around and stuff. I didn't see you at orientation, but it was pretty crazy. This school seems to get bigger every year."

Molly looked at Lucy. She seemed nice. "Molly Stewart," she said, introducing herself. She even managed a smile.

"I'm in seventh grade, but we might have some classes together. At least I can show you where to go," Lucy informed her. Then she seemed to notice her surroundings. "Wow. Nice room. I heard you had a single."

Molly didn't know what to say, but at that moment Mr. Tibbs popped out from under the bed and started to scamper toward the open door.

"Oh, watch it!" Molly cried, running forward to slam the door shut. Mr. Tibbs skidded to a stop, then began to wash his paw casually, as if he hadn't actually been running for the door at all.

"A cat?" Lucy Axminster sounded amazed.

Picking up Mr. Tibbs, Molly carried him over to Lucy. "My dad knew I'd be lonely, so he made a deal with Ms. Thacker to let me have Mr. Tibbs."

"Whoa," Lucy said. "Color me impressed."

Molly grinned, and Lucy grinned back at her. From far below them, they heard a gong chime three times.

25

"Oh, no, classes!" Lucy said, looking flustered. "We'd better go or we'll get demerits. Come on!"

Molly plunked Mr. Tibbs down on her bed, then raced out of her room behind Lucy. And so her first day at Glenmore without her father began.

Classes were held in the school building, which was across the courtyard from the girls' dorm. There were four main buildings at Glenmore, arranged in a big square. In the middle of the square was a swimming pool with a fence around it, and a grassy playing field. Covered walkways led between the buildings in case of rain or snow.

Molly and Lucy ran out of the girls' dorm toward the school building. Lucy pointed as they pounded along the path. "Boys' dorm," she panted. "The low building is the gym and the auditorium. That's where we put on plays and stuff. Hold dances."

Molly raised her eyebrows in interest. She had never been in a school play or been to a dance. Maybe Glenmore wouldn't be so bad after all.

In the school building Lucy took Molly to a classroom. "This is your homeroom, since your name starts with S. I have to go to my own homeroom now, but I can meet you during water break at ten-thirty." She pointed to a water fountain at the end of the hall. Then with a friendly smile she said, "See you later, Molly. Good luck."

Molly smiled back. "Thanks. Thanks for your help."

"No prob," Lucy said, and headed down the hall toward some stairs.

Inside the classroom about twenty sixth-grade kids, both boys and girls, were already sitting at desks. From orientation, Molly remembered that no girls were allowed in the boys' dorm, and no boys were allowed in the girls' dorm, but boys and girls ate together and took classes together.

Molly knew everyone there had to be new, too, since they were in sixth grade, but some of them were pretending to be casually bored. Or at least Molly assumed they were pretending.

She found a seat toward the back of the classroom and sat down. An Asian boy sitting next to her gave her a nervous smile. Molly smiled back. To kill time until the teacher came, Molly studied her class-mates, making mental notes about them that she would put into her journal later.

A cheerful-looking plump woman, with her hair in a fuzzy bun on top of her head, came into the room.

"Good morning, class," she said. "My name is Mrs. Newman. If you're in this classroom, you should be in sixth grade, and have a last name that begins with a letter from *M* to *Z*. Is everyone supposed to be here?" No one got up to leave, so Mrs. Newman continued. "When I call your name, come up to my desk and get your class schedule."

The first day passed very quickly. All the sixth-grade classes were on the first floor of the school building, except for science, history, and math, which were on the second floor. It was pretty easy for Molly to find her way around.

In the middle of the morning, after English and history, there was a ten-minute recess so that students could get a drink of water or change books at their lockers. As promised, Lucy met Molly at the water fountain, and showed her where the girls' bathroom was. She seemed to know all of the older students by name, and she pointed out a few of them to Molly.

"That's William Bixter," she whispered, pointing to a cute African-American boy with huge brown eyes. "He's in eighth grade, and he thinks he's the best thing that ever happened to Glenmore. Last year an eighth-grade girl actually asked him to be her date for the Christmas dance, and he was only a junior then. Now his head is so swollen he can barely fit through the doors."

Molly giggled.

"That's Celeste Foucher," Lucy said, pointing to a very pretty older girl. "She's the girl version of Willy Bixter. I can't stand her."

Celeste had blond curly hair and was wearing makeup. She had on a short plaid skirt and a boy's shirt with the ends knotted at her waist. She was popping gum.

"Where did you go to school before this?" Molly asked Lucy.

"A girls' school called Mary Rye," Lucy answered. "Actually, a lot of girls who go there end up here for middle school. And a lot of the boys come from the James Bell Academy. So some of us have known each other for years. And after this a lot of us will probably end up at Foxcroft or someplace like that."

Molly thought it was strange for kids to head off to boarding school when they were little. It made her wonder why their parents had bothered having children in the first place.

"Like, over there," Lucy said, pointing. "That's Rebecca Hirschman."

"I met her yesterday," Molly said.

"Uh-huh. She's in sixth grade, so she's a new girl, but I've known her since she was in second grade and I was in third."

"You both went to Mary Rye?"

"Yep. And she started at Mary Rye in kindergarten. Her folks just dropped her off, and I don't think she's seen them that much since then."

Molly looked at Lucy. "That's awful." She thought about how much her own father must be missing her, and how much she missed him. It would be unbearable to be separated for years.

"Oh, it's not that unusual," Lucy said cheerfully. "I mean, my folks are always thrilled when I leave again for school. During vacation they never know what to do with me."

While Molly glanced at Lucy to see if she was

29

serious, Mrs. Newman came into the hall and rang a small silver bell. "Okay, students," she said. "It's time for the Group A music class. Please check your class cards to see if you're Group A."

"Music classes are mixed-grade," Lucy explained as they checked their class cards. "I'm Group A. What about you?"

"Yeah," Molly said happily. "Me too." She was glad that she and Lucy would have at least one class together. Already she felt that they could be friends—Lucy was so nice and down-to-earth. Not stuck-up like some of the other kids she had met.

Mrs. Newman clapped her hands. "Okay, students. Please line up in pairs and walk quietly to the music room. Travis, please stop pushing."

Feeling almost like a captive in a bizarre prison, Molly took her place next to Lucy and they began to march down the hall. Some of the boys were cutting up, but they weren't making too much noise.

The music room was across the yard in the same building as the gym and the auditorium. It was pretty fancy, Molly realized as they walked in. The music room was large, with about sixty chairs lined up in rows before a small wooden stage. On the stage there was a beautiful piano, and off to one side was an expensive stereo system. Molly glanced around and counted six large speakers in the room.

"Do you play an instrument?" Lucy asked as they waited for the teacher to arrive.

"I can sort of play the piano," Molly told her. "I never had any lessons, though."

"Well, if you want private lessons you can talk to Mr. Destin, the teacher," Lucy said. She grinned. "We call him Mr. Destiny, because he's adorable."

Molly grinned back.

"These classes are mostly music appreciation," Lucy informed her. "I take private lessons for violin." She made a face. "I stink."

Molly laughed. Then Mr. Destin came in and everyone was quiet. *Lucy was right,* Molly thought. *Mr. Destin is really cute. Okay, one cute teacher, one good friend. I'm doing all right so far, Dad.*

At lunchtime Molly collected her tray and got in line. The dining room was large with tall French windows looking out over the courtyard. It had patterned carpet on the floor and long red velvet curtains at the windows. Row after row of shiny wooden tables, each with eight chairs, filled the room. Behind a tall wooden screen was the food line, where Molly was. She pushed her tray along the shelf and picked what she wanted to eat.

Searching the crowd with her eyes, Molly spotted Lucy waving for her to come sit at her table.

"On special occasions we get waited on," Lucy said. "But usually it's cafeteria-style."

"You mean waiters come in just to serve us?" Molly asked.

"Actually," Lucy said with a grin, "usually it's the freshmen who do the serving. But at least you'll only be a freshman one year."

Molly laughed, picturing herself rushing back and forth to the kitchen with heavy trays. "Did you have to do it last year?"

Lucy nodded. "Twice."

"Oh, geez," Molly said, taking a sip of milk. She wondered how many other boarding school traditions she was going to find out about.

"Could you please pass the salt?" A girl with wavy, medium-brown hair to her shoulders gestured to the saltshaker in front of Molly.

Molly pushed it over to her. "I'm Molly Stewart," she said.

"Shannon O'Torr," the girl said shyly. "Are you an old girl?"

Molly shook her head. "Sixth grade. This is Lucy Axminster—she's showing me around. What about you?"

Shannon and Lucy smiled at each other, then Shannon sighed. "I'm a new girl, too, but the old girl who was assigned to me has kind of ditched me."

"Who was it?" Lucy asked.

"Um . . ." Shannon looked around. "That's her. Melissa Sanders." Shannon looked embarrassed.

"It's not your fault she ditched you," Lucy said kindly. "Sometimes old girls do that—they just don't want to be bothered. Don't worry about it.

32

Molly here is getting to know her way around, and you can hang with us, if you want."

Molly gave Lucy a grateful smile. *Lucy is so nice,* she thought. *I really lucked out.*

Shannon also smiled at Lucy. "Thanks," she said. "It's kind of overwhelming being here, away from my parents and all." Then she frowned and looked embarrassed again, as if she shouldn't have admitted it.

"I feel the same way," Molly told her, and Shannon looked much happier. "But the three of us will stick together, and it'll be okay." *At least, I hope it will.*

Later Molly and Shannon found they were in the same composition class, and they sat next to each other. And at dinnertime Molly, Lucy, and Shannon all sat together. Lucy introduced them to some other friends of hers, including a couple of boys, and after dinner they hung out in the junior lounge and talked.

Then it was study period, which was from eight-thirty to nine-thirty every night, when students had to stay in their own rooms and do their homework.

When Molly got back to her room, Mr. Tibbs was asleep on top of the small TV her father had arranged for her to have. Lucy had been shocked when she heard about it—no one else was allowed to have TVs. They all had to share the ones in the junior and senior lounges, and the game room, which was on the first floor of the boys' dorm.

Molly picked up the kitten and cuddled him against her. "Hey, boy," she said softly. "Did you eat your dinner? I missed you today." Mr. Tibbs slowly uncurled himself, then wiggled out of Molly's arms and slid down onto the bed. Seeing a catnip mouse there, he immediately slunk down on his belly, creeping up on it. Then with a fierce leap he pounced on it, grabbing it with his front paws and kicking with his back feet. Molly cracked up.

That night, right before lights out at ten o'clock, Molly wrote in her journal. She described Lucy and Shannon, and wrote down everything she remembered about her first day at Glenmore.

. . . and as soon as I have some time, I'm going to write a long letter to Dad. So far Glenmore seems okay, and I'm so glad to have met Lucy and Shannon. But something in me just can't believe how long it will be till Dad and I are together again.

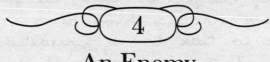

An Enemy

September 10

Dear Dad,

I've been at Glenmore two weeks now, and just got your first letter. So I guess it took almost two weeks to get here. It looked kind of beat-up.

Things here are okay. I've made two friends: Lucy Axminster and Shannon O'Tou. Shannon is a scholarship student, and there are some jerky kids here who call her Shannon O'Poor behind her back. Which I think stinks. But she's really nice.

Besides missing you, I'm doing okay. Mr. Tibbs is fine. I love having him. He's very good to talk to. He shredded part of the window seat, but I flipped the cushion over and no one's noticed yet.

Lucy's father is taking her to the horse show at Boston Garden next week. She says I can go too! I can't wait. I'll spend that weekend at her parents' house.

Well, Dad, I'd better go. The dinner bell is about to ring, and I'm starving. The food here is pretty decent.

You know I miss you, right? I do. Tons and tons. And I love you, too. I hope your crew is getting settled, and that your movie is going okay. Write or call when you can.

Love always,
Molly XXXXXOOOOOO

One morning in mid-September Lucy, Molly, and Shannon found three seats together at breakfast. Breakfast and lunch were always free seating, which meant that kids could sit wherever they wanted. But it was still good to get there early, because everyone always wanted the tables by the windows. Sometimes if you didn't hurry you couldn't find seats together, and then you'd have to split up or, worse, sit at a table with boys. Molly had learned that it was always best to avoid eating with boys. Even the nicest boys, like Peter Jacobs in her math class and John Lopez from English, seemed to become different creatures when confronted with a plate of mashed potatoes and gravy or a square of Jell-O. Molly didn't understand it, but she accepted it as a fact.

That morning the only three seats together were at a table filled with eighth-graders. Another thing Molly had learned was that very few, if any, of the eighth-graders were nice. They were pretty much all horrible and mean and snotty. Lucy had explained it once. "It took them three years to get to the top, and they're facing starting at the bottom again next year in high school, so they want to get in all their power-grubbing now."

Now Molly and Lucy rolled their eyes at each other and made their way to the last table.

Celeste Foucher blocked Molly from pulling out a chair. "Sorry, kid," she said meanly. "No underlings allowed. Go sit somewhere else."

37

Molly narrowed her eyes. "There *is* nowhere else," she said, trying to make her voice sound cold. She pretended that Celeste was a child star in one of her father's movies. Yeah, she might be the star, but Molly's father was the director/producer. "If there were, I sure wouldn't be sitting next to you by *choice*."

Then Molly plunked her tray down on the table and knocked Celeste's foot off her chair, hard. Lucy sat across from her, and Shannon sat meekly at the end, looking nervous.

"Hey, what day is today?" Lucy asked, ignoring Celeste and the other eighth-graders, who were making faces and holding their noses.

"Um, Tuesday," Molly said, opening her orange juice.

"Riding classes start next week," Lucy said excitedly. "Did your dad sign you up?"

"Yeah," Molly answered, her green eyes shining. "Dad said he was going to make sure I had a pony of my own. He said sometimes the ponies at a stable are kind of run-down."

"Well, the ones at Pink's are all pretty nice," Lucy said, taking a bite of her bacon. "But it's nice you'll have one all to yourself."

Molly turned to Shannon. "Are you going to take riding lessons, too?"

Blushing, Shannon shook her head. "It costs extra," she said softly. "Like private music lessons, and some of the field trips. So I can't do it."

"Why did you even ask her?" Laura Bailey, a friend of Celeste's, asked snidely. "Don't you know you're talking to Shannon O'Poor?"

Shannon blushed even harder and stared at her plate.

"Shut up," Molly said angrily to Laura. She tried to think of something quickly that would put Laura in her place. "You're just jealous 'cause she's pretty and you're a dog," she snapped.

All the conversation around them stopped dead. Molly's face was burning with anger and regret—she couldn't remember ever saying anything so mean in her whole life. Now everyone was staring at her as if she had two heads. Catching Lucy's eye, Molly noticed that Lucy was biting her lip, trying not to smile. So at least Lucy didn't hate her for being so mean.

Shannon was staring at her plate, looking as though she wanted the floor to swallow her up. It was true that with her wavy brown hair, smooth, creamy skin, and large brown eyes, Shannon was pretty. It didn't seem to matter that she didn't have as many clothes as other girls, or that she didn't wear designer labels. And it was also true that Laura, with her fiery red hair, pale gooseberry eyes, and freckles, was a bit on the ugly side. But she was really rich, and her father was a banker, and no one had ever spoken to her that way before.

Molly knew everyone was looking at her, and she picked up her fork and tried to eat, hoping the whole thing would just blow over. Maybe later she would even apologize to Laura. Watching Molly coldly, Laura took a sip of milk. Lucy picked up her spoon and took another bite of oatmeal. Even Shannon, squirming miserably, tried to drink some juice.

Then it started. A boy at a nearby table (Molly didn't know his name yet) leaned back in his chair, threw back his head, and barked—softly at first, and then a little louder.

Molly groaned and dropped her head into her hands. How had this happened? The whole thing was spinning out of control. In her seat, Laura flushed furiously, her face turning a bright red, making her freckles stand out as lighter spots. One hand gripped her fork tightly. Molly knew there was no hope of forgiveness now.

Soon another boy put in a small howl, as though he were baying at the moon. Another boy panted and pretended to scratch at fleas. Someone else barked, and someone else whimpered, pretending to want to go outside.

Laura slammed her milk glass on the table and Molly jumped, sure that the other girl would throw it at her. But then Ms. Thacker strode into the room and clapped her hands. One of the teachers on duty must have alerted her.

"That's enough!" she snapped. Her usually calm and smiling face looked very angry. She clapped her hands again. "Silence, I said!" Everyone quieted down. Ms. Thacker looked around the room, a sharp frown on her face. It was as if she was a whole new person, Molly thought. "The rest of the meal will be quiet. The first person who makes an uncalled-for sound will be sent to my office. Is that clear?"

One hundred and twenty students nodded seriously. Ms. Thacker turned and stalked out of the room. It took a few minutes after she left for people to loosen up again and begin talking in low voices. As soon as she could, Shannon finished her breakfast. After throwing Molly a quick, grateful smile, she excused herself and took her tray back to the bussing station.

Across the table, Lucy nudged Molly's foot gently and gave her a little smile that said, *Don't worry. It'll all blow over.* Molly nodded at her.

"Oh, Molly, we have that art history test on Wednesday," Lucy said out loud. "You want to study together?"

"Sure," Molly said, finding her voice. "We can study in my room after dinner."

"Ah yes, your *single* room," Celeste commented in a low voice, daintily pushing some scrambled egg onto a piece of toast. "Isn't that nice? Except it isn't really a single, is it? Since you have to share it with your *cat*. What's its name? Bibbsey?"

Molly set her jaw. "Mr. Tibbs," she muttered. She knew she was the only student allowed to have a pet. *So sue me.*

"Well! I'm done," Lucy said brightly. "Coming, Mol?"

"Right behind you," Molly said, gulping down

her milk. This had to take the prize as the worst breakfast she'd ever had in her life. And now she had some real enemies: Laura Bailey and Celeste Foucher.

That night Molly and Lucy were in Molly's room, their art history books open in front of them. Molly was in the beanbag chair her father had bought her, and Lucy was sprawled across Molly's bed. Mr. Tibbs was attacking Lucy's shoelaces, and Lucy was wiggling her feet and laughing.

"He's so cute," she said, moving her foot so the kitten would have to leap high for it. "He must be great to have around when you get lonesome."

One of the things Molly had come to like most about Lucy was her honesty. Lucy didn't pretend that everything was wonderful all the time. She didn't pretend that she herself never got lonely or bummed, and she didn't make Molly feel like a sissy if *she* felt lonely or bummed. She was at boarding school: of course she felt icky sometimes, and of course she missed her father all the time. Lucy understood, and it was cool with her.

"Yeah," Molly said. "I'm so glad I have him. I've never had a pet before. We always moved too much."

Lucy nodded. "We have two dogs at home. But they're my mom's dogs, not really mine. In fact," she said with a laugh, "they're not really dogs. They're pugs—more like breathing fashion accessories." She laughed again, and Molly joined in.

"Have I told you that my mom is really beautiful?" Lucy asked suddenly.

Looking up, Molly shook her head.

Lucy sighed. "I know it's hard to believe, looking at me, but she is. She was a fashion model in the early eighties. Now she's thirty-five, but she's still really beautiful. Kind of amazingly beautiful, you know?"

"Huh," Molly said.

"I look like my dad," Lucy said, brushing her short brown hair off her face. "I think it kills her that I don't look like her. But I don't know what I'd do if I looked like my mom. I guess I'd just sit around and stare into a mirror all day. Which is pretty much what she does." She shrugged. "Oh well."

"My mom was really beautiful, too. I don't look much like her, either. She was dark. Want to see a picture of her?"

Lucy nodded, looking interested.

Molly opened her heart locket and leaned close to Lucy.

"She died when I was just a baby," Molly told her. "She was French."

"Wow," Lucy said. "You're right, she is beautiful. But you do look a little like her—your face, kind of."

For a few moments Lucy looked at the picture in the locket, then Molly snapped it shut. Molly suddenly felt a new wave of loneliness come over her—not only for her dad, but for the mother she had never known. She met Lucy's eyes, and saw the sympathy and understanding there.

"Guess we'd better get studying," Molly said, her voice a little raspy.

"Guess so," Lucy said.

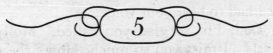

5

Riding Lessons

The very next night Molly was lying on her stomach on the bed, studying. It was almost time for lights out, so she turned down the volume on her CD player. Mr. Tibbs was sitting on the pillow in front of her, and whenever she turned a page he attacked it with his paw. Her history book had tons of tiny holes in its pages.

When the phone on her bedside table rang, she jumped. Her father had paid for her to have her own private line, but no one had called her yet. None of the other students had phones, and most of Molly's friends were back in Taiwan. Now she stared at the ringing phone in alarm.

Then Molly leaped for the nightstand. "Hello?"

"Hey, sweetie," came the voice over the scratchy line. It sounded very far away.

Molly's eyes practically bugged out of her head. "Dad!" she yelled. "Where are you calling from?"

"One of the techies rigged up a cellular phone,"

her father said. "We're far from the nearest radio cell, so I don't know how long this connection will last, but I had to hear your voice."

"Oh, Dad, I'm so glad you called," Molly said breathlessly. "I miss you so much. How's the movie going?"

"It's okay. One of our backers pulled out, so I had to sink more of my own money into it. And then one of our locations got washed away in a hurricane. But other than that, we're hanging in there. How's my little princess doing?"

"I'm fine," Molly said. She was so excited to hear her father's voice that she was hopping from foot to foot around the phone. "Are you getting all my letters?"

"I got one this morning," her dad said. "I guess our letters are going to cross in the mail. It sounds like you're finding your way around all right. Did you have a good time at Lucy's house?"

Molly wrinkled her nose. "Not really," she said honestly. "Her parents don't get along that well, and her mom doesn't seem to like her that much. It actually seemed like her mom liked me more than Lucy. It was weird."

"Yeah, that does sound weird. But you know how strange grown-ups can be."

Molly laughed into the phone. She missed her dad so much! Nobody could cheer her up like he could.

All of a sudden there was a lot of crackling on the line, but Molly heard her father say, "I'd better get off the line, sweetie, before it conks out. I'll write to you, but I just wanted to talk to you for a second."

"I'm glad you called, Dad. I really miss you." Molly felt a lump coming into her throat.

"I miss you, too, honey. Every minute. I can't wait till I see you again."

"Me too." A tear slowly ran down Molly's face.

"Okay, bye, sweetie. I love you."

"I love you, too, Dad."

Then Molly heard a scratchy click, and the dial tone came back. She sat down on her bed, picked up Tibbsey, and let her tears fall into his soft blue-gray fur. "I'm being brave," she told the kitten. "But sometimes even brave people have to cry a little bit."

The last Saturday of September, riding lessons started. Just as with music and art, the classes included both boys and girls of all grades. Molly and Lucy already knew they had lucked out—they were both in Group H. So was Peter Jacobs, whom Molly was becoming friends with. Unfortunately, Celeste Foucher and Laura Bailey were in Group H, too.

The blue and white Glenmore bus took Group H to Pink's and Lytton's, which was a stable close to the large public park. When they got there, everyone lined up in the main indoor ring, waiting to be assigned their ponies. Group G had already dismounted and were climbing on the bus to go back to Glenmore.

Soon everyone had a pony but Molly. Ralph Green, their teacher, said, "You must be Molly Stewart."

Molly nodded.

"Well, your father has arranged for you to have your own pony, Molly," said Mr. Green. He turned and yelled toward the wide hall. "Bobby! Bring out the Stewart pony!"

Turning back to Molly, Mr. Green said, "He'll be stabled here, but no one else will ride him. He'll also be available for you to ride in the afternoons, if you want, and on the weekends."

Then a groom came out leading Molly's pony. Her eyes widened. He was a beautiful pony, with a dark bay coat, black mane, and black tail. She walked toward him and gently ran her hand down his silky neck. "Oh, you're gorgeous," she breathed. "What's his name?" she asked.

"Well, we've been calling him Brownie, but he needs a proper name now," Mr. Green said with a smile. "You need to give him one."

"Okay," Molly said, thinking for a minute. The pony looked back at her proudly, and delicately shifted his hindquarters around. He was at least a hand bigger than the class's other ponies, and he seemed somehow more elegant—bolder, yet more refined. Suddenly she had his name. "Montana," she said. "Your name is Montana. Because you're so big and beautiful."

The pony bobbed his finely molded head and whinnied softly, as if in approval. Laughing, Molly threw her arms around his neck. "Montana, you're fabulous! I love you!"

While the groom held him, Molly carefully put on the new saddle her father had bought her at a Boston leather store. Montana waited patiently while Molly swung up into the saddle. Then she edged him over to stand in line with the rest of Group H. Lucy met her eyes and gave her a thumbs-up. Peter Jacobs whistled admiringly.

"What a nice daddy the little princess has," Laura said snidely to Celeste, making sure that Molly could hear her.

Molly flushed but turned away, determined not to let them get to her. Montana was gorgeous, it was a beautiful day, and nothing could stop her from having a good time.

"Okay, Group H," Mr. Green said, motioning them toward the exit. "We're going to move outside into the big ring, where you'll trot and canter in a circle to review what you already know. Anyone having trouble, just give a yell."

With her shoulders back and chin high, the way she had been taught, Molly sat proudly in Montana's saddle and waited for her turn to exit the indoor ring. She couldn't wait to get home and write her father a long letter, thanking him for the best present ever.

On Sunday mornings Molly usually cleaned her room and did her laundry. Of course there were housekeepers who vacuumed and scrubbed the tub and stuff, but Molly still had to put her things away and clean Mr. Tibbs's box.

One Sunday at the end of September, Molly decided to do laundry. She bundled the clothes into her laundry bag, gathered up her journal and a bunch of quarters, and took the elevator to the basement.

There was one other girl down there, a seventh-grader whose name Molly had forgotten. She and the girl exchanged smiles, and Molly started her clothes in two machines. Then she settled in a plastic chair, opened her journal, and began to write. The other girl sat on top of a dryer nearby and pulled out a fashion magazine and a piece of bubble gum. They sat in the warm, damp air of the laundry room with the comforting sounds of whirring washers all around them.

Dear Journal,

I have decided to pretend that I'm at Glenmore doing research for a book about boarding schools. I think it will be easier to bear being away from Dad if I pretend I'm here on a mission, doing work. Maybe Dad will make a *movie about a boarding school one day, and I have to be able to tell him all about it.*

Molly pushed her long blond hair over her shoulder and took a sip of her diet Coke. There was no dress code on the weekends, unless there was a special school function, and she was wearing a dark-blue Glenmore sweatshirt, a pair of jeans, and sneakers.

I feel better already, Journal. I'm just going to pretend —

"You idiot!"

The harsh words made Molly jump, and she almost spilled her can of soda. The girl on the dryer also looked up, startled.

Molly looked around but didn't see anyone else there. Where had the voice come from?

"I—I'm sorry, Ms. Thacker," another, softer voice answered.

"Sorry doesn't cut it, Deborah!" Ms. Thacker snapped. Molly had never heard her sound so angry—not even that day at breakfast. Whenever Molly spoke to Ms. Thacker, the headmistress was always really nice and smiled a lot.

The other girl in the laundry room caught Molly's

51

eye and pointed overhead. There was an old-fashioned hot-air register in the ceiling above their heads. Molly quickly calculated where the laundry room was, and she figured it must be right under Ms. Thacker's office.

"Thanks to your stupid mistake, over forty fund-raising letters did *not* go out to alumni on time for our annual school drive."

"I'm sorry, Ms. Thacker, but I thought you said—"

"Thought! You thought! I don't pay you to think, I pay you to do what I tell you to do!"

Molly and the other girl stared at each other. Ms. Thacker was being so hateful—and all over a bunch of dumb letters.

Ms. Thacker continued, her voice high and nasty, "This run-down hovel needs every penny we can get just to keep going! It's not enough to get students whose parents have more money than brains. We need continued support from ex-students or we're all in the poorhouse! Do you understand?"

From the muffled sounds coming through the register, it sounded as if Deborah, Ms. Thacker's assistant, was crying. Molly didn't know what to think. Glenmore was hardly a run-down hovel—it was kept up better than some five-star hotels. And what did Ms. Thacker mean by parents with more money than brains?

"I'm sorry . . ." Deborah wept.

A new voice joined the scene: Mr. Thacker's.

"Cathy, honey," he said gently, "it wasn't so bad. We're doing really well this year. Tuitions have never been higher, and some of these folks are really paying through the nose. Don't take it out on poor Deborah."

"Oh, Jerry," Ms. Thacker snapped, "just butt out, will you? You know you don't understand the school business. Just let me handle things, okay?"

"But honey—"

"Don't honey me," said Ms. Thacker. "If I left it up to you you'd run this school into the ground in six months. You just don't have a head for business. Now listen, Deborah," she went on, "I don't have time for these kinds of stupid mistakes. From now on you do what I tell you—exactly what I tell you, and nothing else—or you're out on your can. You got it?"

More muffled crying from Deborah.

There was the sound of a door slamming, and then everything was quiet.

Shocked, Molly automatically went and transferred her clothes from the washers into some dryers, and started the dryers.

The other girl stood at a dryer next to her.

"Wow," she said. "I'd heard about it, but I hadn't seen it yet."

"Seen what?" Molly asked.

"Everyone says, all the older girls, that Ms. Thacker is a real rhymes-with-witch," the girl told her. "They say she goes through assistants like used tissues, and that she makes everyone cry. She's even made some of the teachers cry."

"No!" Molly said. "Really?" She couldn't believe it. Ms. Thacker had always been so nice to her. But that had definitely been Ms. Thacker's voice coming through the register.

Later that night, Molly asked Lucy about it.

"Oh, sure," Lucy said casually. "Everyone knows about it. She's always totally sappy with the parents, 'cause they pay the bills, and she's really nice to the richest students. Like you," Lucy said matter-of-factly. "And me. But she's not nearly so nice to Shannon, or to the other scholarship students."

"Really?" Molly still felt shocked. "Shannon hasn't said anything about it."

"You know Shannon. She doesn't exactly stand up for herself. Hey, my dad sent me a new Blue Waverino CD. Want to listen to it?"

"Um, yeah, okay," Molly said. "Mind if I write in my journal while we listen? I want to make a note of everything you just told me."

"Go ahead," Lucy said, waving her hand. "I'll read my new *Baby-sitters Club* book."

So Molly flopped down on Lucy's roommate's bed, and wrote in her journal until the lights-out bell rang.

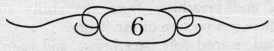

6

The Great Escape

"You look under the bed," Molly instructed Lucy. "I'll look in the bathroom again. Shannon, could you check the closet, please?"

"Okay," Shannon agreed, opening the closet door. She leaned in, pushing aside clothes and shoes. "Here, Tibbsey, here, boy."

In the bathroom Molly checked in the tub and behind the toilet. No sign of pointed blue-gray ears; no small lavender nose peeking out from behind a cupboard.

It was almost dinnertime on a Sunday in early October, just a week after the laundry room incident. Molly, Lucy, and Shannon had all gone riding together in the nearby park. Shannon had borrowed one of Lucy's friends' ponies.

The more Molly rode Montana, the more she enjoyed it. Montana was a wonderful, fabulous pony— fast, nimble, and gorgeous. Since Molly wasn't that great at the team sports they played in p.e., she was glad to get some real exercise riding in the park. But when she had returned to her room, red-cheeked and breathless from the chilly autumn wind, there was no sign of Mr. Tibbs.

He had escaped only once before, and hadn't gotten very far that time. Molly had pounced on him at the top of the steps, just as he was heading downstairs. But this time there was no telling how long he had been gone—he might even have gotten out when she'd left her room to go riding several hours before.

"Here, Tibbsey," she called. "Here, boy. Come on, dinnertime." Picking up a can of cat food, she hit it lightly with a spoon. If he was within hearing, he would come running. But he didn't.

Finally Lucy collapsed on Molly's bed. "Face it, Mol, he's not in this room. But he must be somewhere in the dorm. We should split up and try to find him."

"How can we look for him without anyone finding out?" Shannon asked, brushing her tangled brown hair off her face. "If we wander through the school calling him, everyone will know."

Molly groaned and unbuttoned her riding jacket. "This is all I need. If Ms. Thacker finds out, she's going to kill me. Peter said he overheard her complaining to Augustus about the price of cat food." Augustus Bloch was Glenmore's cook.

"What's she complaining about?" Shannon said impatiently. "We all know she doesn't pay for it—your dad does."

"Yeah," said Lucy. "Anyway, she wouldn't kill *you*. Your dad gave too much money to the school."

Molly made a face at her. After the laundry room incident, she wasn't too sure Ms. Thacker could control her anger, even at Molly. "Well, we have to find him soon—before anyone else does. No matter what."

In the end they decided they would all look together. If anyone asked, they were searching for Lucy's birthstone ring.

By dinnertime they had searched the entire girls' dorm. They didn't actually go into all the rooms, but they figured that if anyone had found Mr. Tibbs, they would have heard about it.

"Could he have gotten out of the dorm?" Molly gasped, leaning against the elevator door.

"Yeah," Lucy said thoughtfully, pushing her mousy hair behind her ears. "If he was waiting by the door right as someone opened it."

"Oh, no," Molly moaned. The school was huge—how would she ever find him? And worse—what if he had gotten *outside*? It was really cold out, and he would get lost, and . . .

Then the dinner gong rang, and they had to stop the search for a while. All students absolutely *had* to show up for dinner on time. Molly dragged herself into the dining hall only to find that it was Italian night.

Every couple of weeks, the kitchen staff threw a theme banquet. The last one had been Chinese night, with Chinese food, paper lanterns, and Chinese music being piped in. This time there were tricolored Italian flags everywhere, and there was an actual accordion player wandering around playing songs.

"Ah, here you are," said Maura Richardson when Molly and Shannon walked in. "Freshmen! Put on these aprons. You're serving tonight."

Just then, Ms. Thacker appeared. The headmistress frowned when she saw Molly tying on the apron. "Maura!" she said sternly. "Molly shouldn't be serving food."

"But—" Maura protested.

"You have plenty of other freshman servers," Ms. Thacker cut in. "I'm sure Molly's father wouldn't be happy to hear that she was forced to work in the kitchen. Run along, Molly." Ms. Thacker swept away before Molly could protest.

With an apologetic shrug at Shannon, Molly went to join Lucy at her table. She sat down next to an eighth-grader. There were also three boys at the table. Molly smiled. No one was going to have an easy night.

Molly watched the freshman servers take large platters of pasta, salad, and rolls from the kitchen to the tables. She felt bad for them—all the seventh- and eighth-graders teased the servers and kept asking for more water or milk or rolls. Molly wondered if her friends were mad at her for not serving.

Sometimes she wished Ms. Thacker wouldn't give her special treatment—it got kind of embarrassing. After a while, Shannon and Peter Jacobs collapsed next to her, looking tired from carrying all that food.

"'Glenmore trains young minds for their roles later in life,'" Shannon quoted from the school pamphlet. "Yeah, it trains you to be a waitress." With a frown, she took a bite of lasagna.

"Or a waiter," Peter Jacobs said from across the table.

Molly didn't know what to say. It really wasn't fair that her friends had to work and she didn't. But she had no time to think about that now. Mr. Tibbs was still missing. She simply *had* to find her kitten as soon as possible.

Molly wolfed down her food as fast as she could. "I've got to go find Mr. Tibbs," she whispered to Shannon.

"But Molly," Shannon began in a low voice, "we can't leave the dining hall until dinner's officially over."

With a regretful shrug Molly ducked out the back door.

Trying to be inconspicuous, and hoping everyone would stay in the dining hall for a little while longer, Molly slunk through the halls of the main building, calling, "Mr. Tibbs! Mr. Tibbs!" in a low whisper. She searched the foyer, the fancy parlor, the nurse's station, and all the administration offices.

She turned down a hall that led to the elevators.

59

Upstairs were all the girls' bedrooms, but on the first floor were the kitchen and storerooms.

Lucy snuck up behind Molly. "Shannon's still bussing tables," she whispered. "Have you done the other rooms yet?"

Molly nodded. "Lucy, what are we going to do? And I had a worse thought: what if someone took him? Like, what if Celeste or Laura found him, and now they're just waiting to use him to get me in trouble?" Molly didn't know what her dad would say if she really got into serious trouble. She knew he would support her and be on her side—that wasn't the problem. But he might have to find another school for her, or fly back to deal with it. He sure wouldn't be happy about that.

"Should we check in the kitchen?" Lucy asked nervously. Students weren't allowed in the kitchen under any circumstances. Augustus, the German cook, was very moody, and had a fierce temper. Going in the kitchen was like taking your life in your hands. Not to mention what would happen if Ms. Thacker found out. *Mucho* demerits.

As the girls were debating the prickly problem the double kitchen doors suddenly swung wide open. A gust of warm air, scented with the mouthwatering smell of baking bread, brushed across their faces. There was a quick glimpse of several white-hatted assistants bustling back and forth, and of an enormous stove with huge flames leaping off a burner.

Then there was Augustus. He stood in front of the two girls, who were struck dumb with surprise and fear. Augustus Bloch was a huge man, well over six feet and two hundred pounds. He had a big, round, red face and an enormous red mustache that curled up at the ends. Now he stood, tall and terrible, arms crossed over his chest, staring down at Lucy and Molly.

Molly swallowed hard. "That was a great dinner, Mr. Bloch," she said in a faltering voice. "The lasagna was fabulous."

"Vat are you girls doing hanging around de kitchen doors?" he asked in a gruff, heavily accented voice.

"We're . . . we're looking for something," Molly said meekly.

"Something? Vat something?" Augustus demanded.

Molly quickly looked around to make sure no one was listening. "Ah, um . . . uh . . . a kitten," she confessed. "A small gray kitten." Then she braced herself for the cook's thundering, outraged response.

"A kitten like dis?" Augustus reached inside his chef's jacket and plucked Mr. Tibbs from within the folds. The kitten hung unconcernedly from the cook's huge red hand. He mewed when he saw Molly.

Molly's eyes almost popped out of her head. Mr. Tibbs! In the kitchen! *Omigosh. I bet Augustus is going to cook him,* Molly thought frantically. *We're going to have cat chops for breakfast.*

"Mr. Tibbs!" Lucy gasped. "Oh, Mr. Bloch, we're so sorry!"

"He's my cat," Molly said bravely. "Lucy didn't have anything to do with it. It's all my fault."

"I found dis animal in front of the refrigerator," Augustus said. "When I open de door, he jump in. So I close de door, to teach him a lesson."

Against her will, Molly drew in a quick breath. The thought of sweet Mr. Tibbs, just a baby still, being shut inside a freezing, dark fridge!

"When I open de door, he is dere, eating a cold baked potato."

Molly's startled green eyes met Augustus's brown ones. "He—he was eating a potato?"

Then Augustus's eyes twinkled, and crinkled at the edges. The next minute he was laughing, holding Mr. Tibbs against his chest.

After a few seconds of staring at each other in disbelief, Molly and Lucy broke into laughter, too.

"Dis little cat, he is very gutsy," Augustus said, scratching Mr. Tibbs's head. "Den, when I put him on de floor, he catch a mouse."

"He what?" Molly shrieked.

"De kitchen has mice. Dis little cat, he caught one. Bam, bam! Two seconds."

"Oh my gosh," Molly breathed. "I can't believe it." She looked at Lucy. "It's like he's been living this secret double life. I'm so sorry he bothered you, Mr. Bloch," Molly said, reaching out her hands for the kitten. The cook gave him to her. "I don't know how he got out, but I'll make sure he'll never do it again."

"No, little girl, dat's okay. I want to——"

"Girls! Surely you aren't bothering Mr. Bloch!" Ms. Thacker's angry voice broke into their conversation.

Quickly Molly shoved Mr. Tibbs inside her riding jacket and crossed her arms over him against her chest. *You'd better not make a sound,* she warned him silently.

Ms. Thacker strode up, frowning, but when she saw Molly her face smoothed into a smile. Looking carefully, Molly saw that the smile didn't go all the way to Ms. Thacker's eyes.

"Oh, it's you, Molly," Ms. Thacker said in a softer voice. "I didn't realize it at first. I should have recognized that pretty blond hair of yours." She smiled again, and Molly forced herself to smile back.

"Listen, dear," the headmistress continued, "let's leave Mr. Bloch alone, shall we? It isn't right to disturb him when he's working so hard." Ms. Thacker placed a gentle hand on Molly's shoulder. Molly tightened her arms around Mr. Tibbs, praying he wouldn't squirm.

"No, is okay, Ms. Thacker," said Mr. Bloch. "Is no problem."

"Well, aren't you nice, Mr. Bloch," said Ms.

Thacker sweetly. "But I can't have the students disturbing you. Girls, I believe Mrs. Newman has a special film presentation for this evening. It's being set up in the senior lounge, okay?"

"Yes, Ms. Thacker," Molly and Lucy chorused.

With another smile, the headmistress turned and headed back into her office.

As soon as she was out of sight Molly said, "We have to go, Mr. Bloch. But thank you very much for finding Mr. Tibbs."

"Listen, little girl. Like I said, de kitchen has mice. Maybe you let me borrow de little cat once a week? He come play in de kitchen, and bam! He take care of mice. Okay?"

"You want to borrow Mr. Tibbs?" Molly smiled as the kitten poked his head out of her jacket. He began squirming to get away, but she held him close. "I guess that would be okay. Catching mice isn't dangerous for him, is it? He's had all his shots."

"He'll be fine," Mr. Bloch assured her. "And I give him special treats."

"Okay," Molly agreed, thinking this was a funny bargain. "I'll sneak him down here next Wednesday, before class."

"Deal." Mr. Bloch put out a huge, meaty hand and shook her small one firmly. Then he swept back into his domain and started barking orders at his assistants.

Molly and Lucy couldn't hold in their giggles as

64

they ran down the hall, then upstairs to Molly's room, with Mr. Tibbs still stuffed inside Molly's jacket. Once in Molly's room, they closed the door carefully and locked it, then let the kitten out.

Flopping on Molly's bed, Lucy cried, "A cold baked potato! I don't believe it! We almost got in so much trouble." She started laughing and bouncing her feet on the bed.

"He's so bad," Molly said, chuckling. "Tibbsey, you are so bad!" She picked him up again and kissed his head. He mewed right in her face. "Ew! Mouse breath! Mouse breath!" Molly cried, dropping him onto the bed again.

Mr. Tibbs refused to look repentant.

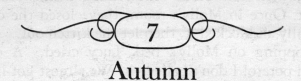

7

Autumn

By mid-October Molly had to dress warmly every day. One Saturday, when she was taking her usual weekend ride in the park, she noticed that the leaves on the trees were changing color. The week before, they had been pale green and yellow. Now the park was filled with glorious bursts of red and orange. For a few moments she slowed Montana to a walk, and just gazed overhead.

Lucy pulled up beside her on her usual pony, a pretty roan mare named Tinker. "Is something wrong?" Lucy panted. Despite being a little plump and not very good at most sports, Lucy had been riding almost as long as she had been walking, and was a much better equestrienne than Molly. Molly always tried to imitate Lucy's form when they were out together.

"No," Molly answered. "It's just so beautiful." She waved her arms overhead, trying to express herself. "The wind, the colors of the leaves—it's fabulous. I haven't lived anywhere where this happens. I'll have to write Dad and tell him how pretty it is."

Lucy looked around. "I'm used to it, but yeah, it is really pretty. It makes you want to go home and curl up with some hot chocolate and a good book."

"Yeah," Molly agreed, smiling at her friend. "But first we have to race back to the stables!" Before Lucy could respond, Molly had lightly touched her heels against Montana's sleek sides, and the pony leaped forward in an eager canter.

"Hey, wait up!" Lucy called behind them. "No fair!"

Laughing, Molly hunched low over Montana's withers, loving the exhilaration of running fast over hilly paths, feeling the chill wind whipping against her face, her long braid flying out in back of her.

October 26

Dear Dad,
    They think it might snow
here tonight. I'm so excited —
I haven't seen snow since
I was five.
    Something weird happened
today. Ms. Thacker called me
into her office and said that
she'd been trying to write to

you but hadn't gotten a
reply. I said that it took a
long time. Anyway, she told me
that sometimes people make big
gifts to the school. She asked
me if I thought you would do
that. She said if you thought
I was very happy here you
might feel grateful and want to
give the school money. Then
she said I didn't need to
mention this little talk to
anyone. So of course I had to
tell you right away.

It's weird — when I first
came here I thought she was
really nice, but the more I
see her the less nice I think
she is.

Besides that everything is
fine, except I miss you, miss
you, miss you. We're having a
Halloween costume party. I'm
going to go as a black cat.
We've all been working on

our costumes in art class.

I'd better go — it's almost time for lights out. I love you, Dad, and miss you.

Your own,
Molly

"How does this look?" Molly stepped back from her mirror and gazed critically at the black whiskers she had drawn on her face.

Lucy paused from struggling into her pumpkin costume. "It looks great," she said sincerely. "I love your ears."

"Was Mr. Tibbs surprised to see you?" Shannon asked with a giggle, adjusting her witch's hat.

Molly laughed, too. "No. He just glanced at me as if he thought I finally looked normal." She pulled her long black tail out of the way so she could sit down. It was Halloween night, and almost time for the costume party. The three girls had decided to all get ready together in Molly's room, since she had her own bathroom and there was plenty of space.

"You know the best thing about Halloween?" Lucy asked, painting her face orange. "It means there's only three weeks till Thanksgiving, and seven weeks till Christmas."

Molly and Shannon laughed. "You know it!" Shannon said.

A few minutes later they made their way across the playing field, taking a shortcut to the auditorium, where the party was being held.

"Man, it's cold," Molly said, her teeth chattering. "Let's hurry."

Inside the auditorium, music was blasting. An eighth-grade boy and girl were choosing which CDs to play on the stereo. Two long tables were covered with cookies, fruit, and vegetables with dips. The auditorium was decorated with orange and black balloons, crepe-paper streamers, and cutouts of cats, witches, pumpkins, and goblins. Everyone was talking, laughing, and eating, and some kids were dancing in the middle of the floor.

"This is great!" Molly had to yell to be heard over the music. "I've never been to a school party like this."

Lucy grinned at her. "Yeah, Glenmore has great parties. We always make sure to elect class presidents who know how to throw a bash. Come on, let's get something to eat."

At the refreshments table Molly took an orange-iced cookie, and just as she was chewing her first bite Peter Jacobs asked her to dance. She smiled and nodded, still chewing, and with her cookie in one hand and the other hand holding up her tail, she followed him to the dance floor.

After that the only time she saw Lucy or Shannon was when they happened to be dancing next to her in the middle of the crowd. It was Molly's first boy-girl party, and she was having a great time. After Peter, she danced with John Lopez, then a seventh-grader, then a few guys she didn't know, then Peter again.

Right at nine o'clock the lights blinked on and off, and Mr. Destin, the music teacher, walked onto the stage. Taking a microphone, he said, "Is everyone having a good time?"

"Yeah!" everyone shouted.

"You know what time it is?" he yelled.

"Yeah!" everyone shouted again.

Molly was yelling and jumping up and down with everyone else, and then she noticed that by coincidence, she and Lucy and Shannon had all ended up standing next to each other by the side of the dance floor.

"What time *is* it?" she yelled to Lucy.

"Time for the costume contest!" Lucy yelled back.

Mr. Destin held up a bunch of index cards. "Throughout the evening, the other chaperons and I have been making notes on who has the best costume. And we're ready to announce the winners!"

"Yay!" the crowd screamed.

"Among sixth-graders, the boys' prize goes to . . . Marc Riley!" Mr. Destin called.

A boy came out from the crowd and walked up to the stage. He had made himself a knight costume out of silver-painted papier-mâché. It looked really good.

"For sixth-grade girls, the prize goes to Mariko Tong!"

A pretty Asian girl who was wearing a fabulous

spider costume happily ran up to the stage.

"What did she win?" Molly asked.

"Last year it was gift certificates to Joe Brown's, that ice cream place I took you to last week," Lucy answered.

"Cool," Molly said.

Davina Etheridge and Tommy Chambers won for the seventh-graders, and in eighth grade Willy Bixter and Celeste Foucher won.

Molly groaned. It was true that they were wearing amazing costumes—Willy was an alien and Celeste was dressed as an old-fashioned china doll—but their costumes were store-bought, and obviously really expensive.

"They should give prizes only to people who made their costumes," Molly complained as the music started for the last dance.

"Yeah," Lucy agreed, taking a last chocolate-iced cupcake. "They shouldn't be only for the people who spent the most on their outfits."

"You're just jealous," came a sneering voice in back of them. Molly and Lucy turned to see Laura Bailey, dressed as Snow White. "You're jealous because Celeste looks so great, and you're just a . . . pumpkin. I mean, I can hardly even tell you're wearing a costume."

"Shut up, Laura," Molly began, but Lucy just held up her hand.

"It doesn't matter, Mol," Lucy said, calmly licking

the icing off her fingers. "She's a nobody. Forget her."

Laura's pale eyes widened in rage, but just then a teacher chaperon drifted closer, so she shut her mouth with a snap and stomped off. Molly and Lucy giggled and slapped each other high fives.

"You guys shouldn't fight with her," Shannon said timidly, taking a sip of punch.

"Why not?" Lucy demanded. "She's a jerk. So's Celeste."

"I don't know," Shannon said, hesitating. "They're so popular. Most people like them."

"Most people suck up to them because they're really rich," Molly said pointedly.

Shannon made a face. "It's just . . . I don't think they're so bad. And Celeste did have a great costume."

"Earth to Shannon," Molly said, her eyes wide in disbelief. "They're the ones who were picking on you just a little while ago. They've said so many mean things about you. How can you stand up for them?"

Shannon shrugged, looking embarrassed. "I don't know," she repeated. "Let's just drop it." She moved away to put her cup back on the refreshment table, leaving Molly and Lucy staring after her in bewilderment.

November 13

Dear Dad,
Did you get my letter from

Monday? I never know if you're getting all these letters I write! It's so cold today that I wore a turtleneck and a wool sweater. My friend Lucy teases me because I feel the cold more than people who are used to being in the north.

I've been riding Montana as much as I can — he's the best pony in the world. In riding classes we're starting to learn how to jump. I love it.

Things here are fine. Now that I know where everything is, and how to do everything, I feel a lot more normal. I'm doing okay in all my classes yesterday I got an A- on an English test.

Mr. Tibbs is fine. He's twice as big as when we got him. I had to take him for

his checkup at the vet's. Lucy
helped me go there — we took a
bus. Everything was fine, and
he sent the bill to Ms.
Thacker.

Oh, I almost forgot! Thank
you so much for the fabulous
cashmere scarf! I wear it
whenever I go out. I don't
know how you keep sending
presents from the middle of
the jungle, but I love getting
them.

I'd better finish up — it's
almost time for lights-out. I
hope the movie is going well —
it's too bad you couldn't film
in that place you wanted. But
I know you'll find an even
better place. Have a good
Thanksgiving, Dad. Even
though I won't be right
there with you, you know that
I really am with you, don't
you? Just part of me is here

at Glenmore, and the rest of
me is with you.
Take care and be careful.
I love you,
Molly XXXXOOOOO
and more XXXXXX

"So do you want to come home with me for
Thanksgiving?" Lucy asked Molly as they moved
down the lunch buffet table.

"It's really nice of you to ask me," Molly said,
taking a roll and putting it on her plate. She waited
for Lucy and they headed to their seats.

"But you'd rather have a cavity filled," Lucy said
once they sat down.

"No, it's just . . ." Molly began. She hesitated,
then said, "Maybe your folks would rather have you
all to themselves. They don't get to spend much
time with you, and I'd only be in the way."

"It's okay," Lucy assured her, pouring herself a
glass of milk from the pitcher on the table. "It probably would be better for you to hang out here instead of going to the House of Gloom. They'll
probably just be arguing a lot, as usual, and Mom
will hang out with her friends and ignore me. If I
could get away with it, I would stay here, too."

"Thanks for asking, anyway," Molly told her. Back
in September she had spent the weekend at Lucy's

house, and it had been very uncomfortable—not the house, which was huge and fancy and had anything they could think of to do, but just being around Lucy's parents was hard. Molly couldn't remember a time when she'd had both parents, but she hoped that they had never argued like Lucy's did.

8

Evie

"Susan, is this all the mail that came today?" Ms. Thacker stood in front of her new assistant's desk, a concerned look on her face.

"Yes, ma'am," Susan said. "I sorted it and put it in your in box, as usual." Seeing the frown on her employer's face, she asked hesitantly, "Is something wrong?"

"No," Ms. Thacker said. "It's just—what's today's date? November sixteenth? I've been waiting for a reply from Michael Stewart concerning a matter I wrote to him about. I just haven't heard from him, is all." She looked thoughtful.

Susan shook her head, obviously relieved that she had done nothing wrong. "Well, I'll be on the lookout for anything from him or White Knight Productions," she said. "As soon as I see it I'll bring it to your attention."

"Yes, okay. Thank you." Still frowning, Ms. Thacker went back into her own office and closed the door.

Susan breathed a sigh of relief.

The week before Thanksgiving was midterm week. Molly was doing well in all her classes, except p.e., where the teacher said she needed to make more of an effort.

"Yeah," Molly moaned to Lucy. "More of an effort not to be a total klutz."

One night the three friends were sprawled in Molly's alcove study area with a bowl of popcorn and their textbooks. Since Lucy was a grade ahead of Molly and Shannon, the only classes they had together were music and art history. But since she had already taken their academic classes, she could warn them about what was likely to be on a midterm.

"Be sure to brush up on your maps in both history and geography," she counseled, taking another handful of popcorn. "Ms. Flint is really into those history maps."

"Molly, I can't believe you're staying here for Thanksgiving," Shannon said, leaning against the arm of the love seat. "Won't you be lonesome?"

"Nah," Molly said casually. "I'm sure a couple of other kids will be staying here, too."

"Yeah," Lucy said. "But they aren't your buds—you don't know them. Are you sure you won't change your mind and come home with me for Thanksgiving?"

"No, it's okay," Molly said firmly. "Are you guys going to have relatives over?"

79

Lucy made a face. "I wish. The more people around, the more my folks have to be on their best behavior." She laughed wryly. "But most of my relatives go away for the holidays—like, they go skiing or on a cruise or something. We used to go skiing, too, but now we save it for Christmas or spring break."

"We probably *will* have a bunch of people over," Shannon said. "Everybody brings something to eat, and Mom makes a turkey, and Dad makes the gravy, and all my cousins come over. They always make us sit at a kids' table by ourselves."

"Sounds like fun," Molly said. Most holidays had been just her and her dad in some hotel somewhere. They would get dressed up and go down for the Thanksgiving buffet, and Molly had always thought it was great. But now, listening to Shannon talking, she suddenly realized that she wanted more. *Maybe next year Dad and I will have a little house with a kitchen,* she thought wistfully. *And we could cook a meal together, and have our friends over, like other families.*

"Yeah, it's okay," Shannon said, shrugging one shoulder.

"Well, Mol, if you change your mind and decide you want to risk the House of Gloom, just whistle," Lucy said.

"Okey-dokey," Molly promised.

But Molly didn't change her mind, and a few days before Thanksgiving she waved good-bye to

Lucy as her friend got into a taxi. Shannon's parents had already picked her up.

"Call me!" Lucy shouted as her father bundled her into the cab.

"Okay!" Molly called back, waving. It was a bitterly cold day, and a stinging, icy rain was falling. As soon as the taxi drove away Molly went back inside and ran upstairs to her room. Most of the students had already left, but there would probably be about twenty kids whose parents were traveling or on vacation and couldn't have them at home.

Molly sat on her bed and picked up her journal. Mr. Tibbs immediately jumped onto the bed, too. He purred and curled up against her, then started washing a paw.

Dear Journal,
    It's pretty quiet here with everyone gone. They have "special activities" planned for the kids who stayed, and Augustus promised me he'd make a traditional Thanksgiving Day dinner. (He likes me a lot now that Mr. Tibbs has caught so many mice!) But still, I can't help feeling a

little lonely. This is the first time I've been without Lucy and Shannon since I came to Glenmore.

It's both good and bad, I think. It's good because I won't have to act cheerful if I feel sad, or be friendly if I feel like being alone. It's bad because if I get too lonely, it's just tough. At least I have Mr. Tibbs.

"I'll write another letter to Dad," she told her kitten softly. "That always makes me feel better."

Gently she pushed Mr. Tibbs onto the bed, where he curled up into a tight, fuzzy, blue-gray ball. Then she sat down at her desk, took out her father's last letter to her, and reread it. A lone tear escaped and rolled down her cheek, but she brushed it away. She was helping him by staying at Glenmore and being happy there. She was helping him achieve his dream—he'd said so. Whenever she remembered that, she felt as though she could deal with almost anything.

On Thanksgiving morning Molly was in the large library, idly looking at books. There was a small, cheerful fire in the fireplace, thanks to Mrs. Sampson, the housekeeper. Molly was curled up on one of the small couches, a stack of books by her side. She had always loved to read, and thanks to all the rich ex-Glenmore students who gave the school money, the library had tons of great books.

She was halfway through a funny book called *Tutu Much Ballet* when the door opened and Ms. Thacker came in. Molly quickly took her feet off the arm of the couch and sat up.

"Good morning, Molly," Ms. Thacker said with a warm smile.

"Good morning, Ms. Thacker," Molly said politely. Somehow she just didn't trust Ms. Thacker anymore, but she tried not to show it.

Then Molly saw the girl standing beside the headmistress. She looked about Molly's age, but Molly had never seen her before. Her short, dark hair was cut badly, and her dark eyebrows were pushed up in a frown. In fact, the girl had a totally yucky expression on her face.

"Molly dear," Ms. Thacker said, pushing the girl forward, "this is Eve Lucas. Eve will be joining us here at Glenmore for the rest of the school year. Eve, this is Molly Stewart, one of our best and brightest students. Molly is in sixth grade, just like you."

Molly smiled tentatively at the girl, but Eve just scowled back. She didn't seem like the Glenmore type of student. Molly had noticed that most of the kids at the school tended to be super-polite and smiley, at least in front of adults.

"Molly couldn't be with her family for Thanksgiving," Ms. Thacker continued, "so I thought perhaps you two girls could get to know each other during the holidays. Molly, would you be so kind as to show Eve around our campus?"

"Sure," Molly said, feeling a little wary. The new girl didn't look like she was into the idea at all.

Another big smile from Ms. Thacker. "Thank you so much. I appreciate it. I'll be in my office if you need anything. Don't forget—a special Thanksgiving dinner in the dining hall at six o'clock." Ms. Thacker walked quickly away.

Molly took a deep breath. "Hi," she said cheerfully. The new girl only sneered at her and started walking around the library.

"This place is like a funeral home," Eve said.

Molly raised her eyebrows. Definitely not a typical Glenmore girl. "Just the library, or the whole place?" Molly asked with interest.

With an angry look, Eve said, "The whole place."

Molly laughed. "I guess that explains the lousy food. We dead people aren't that picky."

Eve gave her a startled glance, then put on her sneering face again. "The food's lousy, too?"

"Actually, no," Molly answered truthfully. "The food is one of the best things going here. Especially breakfast. It's like the food in a good hotel."

84

"I wouldn't know," Eve said defensively. "I've never been to a hotel before."

For a whole minute Molly could only stare at the new girl. Never been to a hotel! For someone like Molly, who had lived in hotels practically all her life, this was like saying she had never breathed air before.

"So you've always had a regular house?" Molly asked in awe.

Eve frowned at her, continuing to wander around the library. "Yeah."

"Where?" Molly asked. "I mean, where are you from?"

Eve wheeled to face her, her hands on her hips, her dark eyes blazing. "Okay, let's just get this over with!" she snapped. "I'm from the Fisher projects. My dad took off before I was born. My mom is a drunk, so they put me into foster homes. But this school, Glenmore, gets money from the government if they take on a couple of charity cases. So here I am, stuck on the fifth floor in a closet, like the live-in help. Finally, the name's Evie, not Eve. Any more questions?"

Molly was stunned. Evie was the most interesting girl she'd met since coming to Boston. She was so much more intriguing than just another rich kid from another rich family whose ancestors had come over on the Mayflower. Maybe Thanksgiving vacation was going to be okay after all.

"One more question," Molly finally got out.

"Yeah?" Evie's eyes narrowed threateningly. "Wanna see my cat?"

That evening after dinner, Evie was slumped in Molly's beanbag chair. Molly was lying on her back on the bed, with her feet propped up against the headboard. She was reading *TV Guide* and eating saltwater taffy. Mr. Tibbs was sleeping on Evie's lap.

"Okay," Molly said in a garbled voice. She chewed and swallowed. "Looks like it's nothing but Thanksgiving specials for the rest of the evening. 'Thanksgiving on Walton Mountain,' 'A *Full House* Thanksgiving,' blah, blah, blah. We could go rent a movie. There's a video place about four blocks away." She sat up and pushed the saltwater taffy away violently. "Take this away from me! How can I even eat it after Augustus's dinner? God, I think I'm going to be sick." She lay on her back again and moaned softly, holding her stomach.

"No one forced you to have that second piece of pumpkin pie," Evie pointed out. "I have to admit you were right about the chow. It isn't bad."

"Wait till you taste the waffles on Sunday," Molly mumbled, her eyes closed.

"One question. No, two questions," Evie said, stroking Mr. Tibbs's fur. "Make that three questions."

Molly twisted around so she could look at Evie. "Shoot."

"One, why are you bein' so nice to me?" Evie

86

looked down at the floor, a frown on her face. "Is it be-nice-to-charity-cases week?"

Molly thought for a moment. "Well, Evie," she said in a high-pitched voice, "here at Glenmore we think it's nice to be nice to the nice." She made a smarmy face. Evie couldn't help smiling a little. "No, seriously," Molly said, "why wouldn't I be? We're both stuck here, where we don't want to be. Next question."

Evie looked around the room. "I'm up on the fifth floor in a room like a shoe box, but this must be the best room in the joint. So are you, like, the richest kid in the world or something? I mean, look at all this stuff."

Molly followed Evie's gaze. There was her CD player, and her small TV with a VCR. There was her laptop computer with a color screen, hooked up to a CD-ROM system that allowed her to play all sorts of neat games. She even had a CD containing a whole encyclopedia that she used for book reports. There was a bookshelf full of books and a cupboard full of games. Posters and pictures were hung all over the walls. It was a pretty nice room, and Evie hadn't even seen Molly's clothes yet.

"Well," Molly said, "I guess my dad makes a lot of money. But mostly he bought me all this stuff because he felt bad about us being apart. You know, he misses me, so he sends me stuff."

"Huh," Evie said. "The last question is . . ." She hesitated, then an angry expression crossed her face. "Are the other kids totally stuck-up or what? Think they're going to wash their hands after they meet me?"

"I think it's going to be like any other school," Molly told her honestly. "Some kids will be cool, some won't care one way or another, and some are going to be totally horrible. People might think it's weird that you don't live with the rest of us—I mean, I never even knew there *was* a fifth floor to the girls' dorm. It's like you're living in an attic! So they might treat you differently because you live somewhere different."

Molly thought for a moment. "The thing is," she continued, "there's about a hundred and twenty kids here, so you won't stick out that much. The thing to remember is not to let any of the eighth-graders get to you, because they're all awful and snobby."

"Huh," Evie said again. Then she put her hand on Mr. Tibbs's chest and broke into a smile—the first real one Molly had seen.

"What?" Molly asked.

"He's purring," Evie said, looking amazed.

"Oh," Molly said casually, "he just feels sorry for you 'cause you're a charity case."

Evie stared at Molly, and then they both burst into laughter.

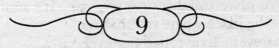

9

The Last Free Day

Over the next few days, Molly hung out with Evie almost all the time. On Saturday they went to a movie, and Molly found out that Evie knew her way around Boston much better than Molly did.

"It's 'cause I've lived here my whole life," Evie pointed out as they walked to the trolley stop. "And I've been on my own a lot."

After the movie they headed to Joe Brown's for ice cream, even though it was freezing out. As they walked Molly pointed out useful places around the neighborhood.

"There's the video store I was telling you about. And over there is a pharmacy where you can get soap and shampoo and stuff. This is a record store, but they're expensive. I usually go to Tower Records, at the mall."

Evie looked at her. "What does it matter if it's a little more expensive? You've got money to burn, right?"

Molly had never thought about that. "Well," she

said slowly, "I guess it really *doesn't* matter, actually. But I don't know—it seems stupid to pay the most expensive price just because you can. It's more fun to go to the place where it's cheaper."

"Whatever." Evie rolled her eyes.

Molly laughed, feeling self-conscious. "Here's Joe Brown's. They have great stuff."

As they sat drinking their hot chocolate Molly watched their reflections in the mirror. Since coming to Glenmore she had felt that most of the kids there, both boys and girls, were pretty much alike, and that she stuck out like a flamingo in a zebra factory. But now she saw to her surprise that she looked a lot more like the rest of the Glenmore kids than Evie did. Evie really did look different somehow. Molly couldn't tell why. Was it just because of money? Was it how she talked? Molly didn't think Evie looked *poor,* exactly. She just seemed to know more about things, to be more aware somehow. Molly decided to write about it in her journal later. Maybe she could figure it out then.

"What do you want to do today?" Molly asked Evie at breakfast on Monday. It was their last full day of vacation: kids would be coming back from vacation the next day, and classes started again on Wednesday.

Evie shrugged, helping herself to more cereal and milk.

"We could go to another movie," Molly suggested, but Evie didn't look thrilled at the idea.

"How about a museum?" Evie said, then shook her head. "I forgot. It's Monday. They're closed."

"Yeah. Well, we could take a walk, or we could go to the stables and take turns riding my pony."

Evie looked up, interested. "I rode a pony once. I liked it. Maybe we should do that."

After breakfast they split up to dress more warmly, then Molly decided to go meet Evie at her room. She'd heard Evie joking about her "cell," but she hadn't seen it yet. She'd never even been to the fifth floor. She didn't know how to get there. Molly was curious to see it.

After taking the elevator to the fourth floor of the girls' dorm, she found a flight of stairs inside what looked like a closet door. A dirty skylight cast a pale-gray light on the narrow, rickety stairs. Molly couldn't believe she was still in Glenmore.

On the fifth floor it was still and quiet. The hallway was narrow and needed painting. Two dim light fixtures in the ceiling made pools of yellow light on the scuffed wooden floor. Tentatively Molly walked down the hallway, wondering if Evie had already gone downstairs. Then she heard Evie's muffled voice, singing softly to herself behind a door.

Molly tapped, and the singing stopped.

The door was pulled open, and Evie stood there, surprised.

91

Then she frowned. "I said I'd meet you down-stairs," she said stiffly.

Molly shrugged. "I thought I'd come meet you up here."

"You just wanted to see how us poor folks live, huh?" Evie said with a sneer. "You were just curious. Admit it." She stood in the doorway, her arms folded across her chest.

"Well, of course I was curious," Molly said patiently. "I didn't even know the fifth floor existed until you told me a few days ago. Wouldn't you be curious?" Without waiting for Evie to reply, Molly continued, "And you know what? You were curious about my room. You walked around and looked at everything and asked me questions. Why is it okay for you to do that but not for me?"

Evie frowned again. Then she unfolded her arms and put a carefully casual expression on her face. "Fine. Come in. Welcome to the Batcave." She flung open the door and stood back, looking defiant.

Molly walked in. Evie's room was small, maybe the size of Molly's small study alcove. It was dark, because the only window was a small rectangular skylight in the ceiling that needed washing. The walls were a dingy gray color, and were scraped and marked from furniture having been moved. Evie's bed looked old and uncomfortable, with a thin mattress and not enough blankets. There was a small, battered desk and a chair held together with string.

An ancient chest of drawers with one drawer missing held Evie's meager supply of clothes.

Molly glanced at her friend. Evie's defiance had faded, and now she was gazing at the floor, looking mortified.

"Get your coat," Molly said. "It's cold outside."

They walked down the stairs, then waited for the elevator.

"I didn't choose my own room, you know," Molly said conversationally. "And you didn't choose yours. So I can't really be proud of my room, and you can't really be ashamed of yours."

"Whatever," Evie said, tapping her foot against the floor. But she didn't look angry anymore.

On the first floor they walked down the hall and through the glass double doors. Ms. Thacker was standing by the receptionist's counter in the foyer. She looked up, but didn't smile until she recognized Molly.

"Molly, you're being very kind to Eve," Ms. Thacker said. "I hope she appreciates your showing her all around."

"Oh, yeah," Evie said in a bored voice. Molly tried not to laugh.

"Eve, I have here an envelope from your patrons," Ms. Thacker said. Molly noticed that somehow all the warmth left Ms. Thacker's voice when she spoke to Evie. "They've very generously given you two hundred dollars to be used on new clothes. The only stipulation is that you get one navy blue blazer, one

93

gray pleated skirt, and one white blouse. After that, you may buy whatever clothes you want, as long as they're suitable for Glenmore, of course."

Evie and Molly stared at each other in delight.

"Want to go shopping with me?" Evie asked Molly.

"Yeah!" Molly said. They slapped high fives.

"How 'bout this?" Evie asked, holding up an oversized waffle-weave sweatshirt at the Gap at Faneuil Hall.

Molly nodded. "Yeah, it's cute. But remember: 'Glenmore girls must look neat and presentable at all times.'" She made a face. "So we actually do need to get some stuff we can wear to class." Her father had bought her lots of clothes before she started at Glenmore, but Molly wanted some new things that weren't so fancy.

"Okay. Look. These leggings, and this tunic top. Will they catch the beady eye of Ms. Thwacker?"

Laughing at the nickname, Molly said, "I think they'll be okay. And that color is really good on you."

Evie stopped to look in a full-length mirror. "Yeah?" She held the top against her. "You know," she said slowly, "I've never had this much money to spend in my life. And I've never had this many new clothes—I mean, clothes that weren't hand-me-downs, or from the thrift shop. It feels kind of weird." Her dark eyes met Molly's green ones.

"I know what you mean," Molly said, coming to stand next to her. "Only opposite. It's always been me and my dad, so this is the first time I've bought clothes for myself, too." She smiled at Evie in the mirror. "I like it."

Finally, at the end of the day, they flopped down on a bench, loaded with bags.

"We'd better be getting back," Molly said tiredly. "It'll be time for dinner pretty soon."

Evie yawned. "Okay. I think we covered everything. We did pretty good, huh? I have only ten dollars left."

At almost the exact same time, their eyes fell on a sign across the mall corridor: SUPERCUTS: ANY HAIRCUT $7.95.

Molly looked at Evie, and Evie looked at Molly.

"That leaves you two dollars for a tip," Molly said.

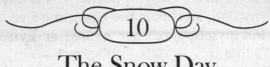

10

The Snow Day

Wednesday morning was December first. When Molly woke up that morning, everything seemed very quiet. Usually she could hear traffic going by on the street below her windows and people talking as they walked to the subway stop on the corner. But that morning everything was muffled and silent.

She got out of bed, carefully disentangling herself from Mr. Tibbs, who had burrowed beneath the covers during the night. Padding over to the window, Molly shivered. It was early, and the heat hadn't come on yet. When she opened her blinds, she gasped. The street outside looked like a scene from a fairy tale.

The last time Molly had seen snow was at least five years before, when she and her dad had been in Canada for the Montreal Film Festival. She had almost forgotten what it looked like. But there it was, covering everything like thick white frosting, deadening sound, making the whole world clean and quiet and wonderful.

Oh, Dad, she thought. *If only you could see this with me. You definitely have to put a snow scene in your next movie.*

At breakfast Molly waited anxiously to introduce Evie to Lucy and Shannon. She had told Lucy about Evie while they were getting their cereal and toast from the buffet, but Evie hadn't come downstairs yet.

Lucy had had a lousy time at home for Thanksgiving. "It's a good thing you weren't there," Lucy told Molly, pouring herself a glass of juice. "I wish I hadn't been."

Molly made a sympathetic face.

Then Evie appeared with her tray, and Molly patted the seat next to her. At almost the same time, Shannon sat down across from Lucy.

"Evie Lucas, this is Lucy Axminster. Lucy's in seventh grade. She saved my life when I first started at Glenmore. And this is Shannon O'Torr. She's in sixth grade, with us."

Evie gave Lucy a cool glance, then sat down. "Did you tell them I was a charity student?" she asked in her familiar angry tones.

Molly rolled her eyes. She'd been hoping Evie wouldn't have to do that with every new person she met. But apparently she did.

Lucy gave Molly an amused look. "Oh, my goodness," she said, putting her hand to her chest. "A charity student? Here at Glenmore? Gosh, could you come

97

with me to my science class so I can look at you under a microscope?" She turned her round blue eyes on Evie and blinked them several times behind her glasses.

For almost thirty seconds Evie just stared at Lucy. Then suddenly her face crinkled into a smile, and she started laughing. Lucy joined her, and soon Molly was laughing, too.

"Okay, okay," Evie said, taking a deep breath. "Fine. Forget I mentioned it."

Molly grinned. But when she looked at Shannon she could see the other girl sitting stiffly in her seat, as though she really did feel that Evie was different. A few minutes later, when both Evie and Lucy had gone back for seconds, Molly asked, "What's wrong, Shannon?"

"Nothing," Shannon said uncomfortably. "It's just—does she have to sit here? I mean, it's bad enough being here on a scholarship without people lumping me into a group with *her*." The words came out in a rush, and afterward Shannon stared unhappily down at her plate while Molly gazed at her in shock.

But there was no time to say anything before Evie and Lucy got back. Molly decided to think about it and talk to Shannon later. For the moment she would pretend that nothing was wrong.

"It's not fair," Lucy was saying bitterly as she sat back down. "Every other school in the city is closed because of the snow, but does Glenmore close? Nooooo."

"That's because our classrooms are part of where we live," Evie said in disgust. "We don't have to commute."

"Really? Schools close when there's snow?" Molly asked.

"Only when there's a lot of snow," Shannon clarified, still focusing her attention on her plate. "When it's just a couple of inches, they don't close. But last night it snowed almost eight inches. That's a lot."

"The schools in the suburbs close before the schools in the city," Lucy said knowledgeably, "because it's impossible for people to drive to them. It's easier in the city, where you can take a subway."

"I remember when I was going to day school," Shannon said. "I was so happy when we had a snow day. Then my mom would stay home from work with me and my brother, and the three of us would play games in front of the fireplace all day."

"That sounds great," Molly said. *Especially the having-a-mother part,* she thought. She'd always been so happy having just her dad around, but for the past three months she had been surrounded by kids her age, and most of them had mothers. Not all of them, but most of them. For the first time, Molly felt envious of other kids. Her father was wonderful, and Molly adored him, but a mother was different, special. Even a mother like Lucy's, who didn't seem much like a mother at all.

As it turned out, the girls got their wish after all. Ms. Thacker came into the dining room after lunch to make an announcement. Mr. Thacker followed her in, and waved to a few of the boy students cheerfully.

"Students," Ms. Thacker said, "I'm afraid that Mr. Destin, Mr. Howard, Ms. Grayson, and several other teachers are unable to reach Glenmore because of the snow."

As the students broke into cheers Ms. Thacker held up a hand. "Just a minute. I know all of you are anxious not to fall behind in your studies," she said impatiently, "so I'm sure you'll be glad to take the next hour as a study hour, during which you will do your lessons independently."

Molly joined the others in heartfelt groans.

"However," Mr. Thacker continued, "because you're all young and healthy, and because we remember what fun it is to play in the snow, after one hour of study you may take the rest of the day off and go outdoors into the playing field only. Don't leave the school campus."

Most of the students shouted and bounced up and down in their seats. Some of the boys whistled and made whooping noises. Most of the eighth-grade girls looked bored.

December 1

Dear Dad,

I had so much fun today.
The only thing that would
have made it better is if
you'd been with me. It snowed!

We all went out and played
in the snow. I wore that cute
ski outfit you sent just a
few days ago. It fit perfectly!
Lucy, Evie, Shannon, and me,
I mean I, made snowballs
and a snowwoman, and I
even made a snowcat.

You know what, Dad? Even
though I miss you so much
all the time, and it's like a
big pain in my heart, still,
this is the first time that
I've had a lot of kids to
play with. The kids at the
American School in Taiwan were
nice, but somehow it wasn't
the same. I really like having
Lucy and Evie and Shannon

101

and some of the other kids
just to hang out with. It's
fun!

All the same, Dad, I'll be
so, so, so happy when you
come back and we can be
together.

I have to go. Mr. Tibbs is
yowling for his dinner.

I love you so much, and
miss you so much.

Your own,
Molly

P.S. I'm mailing your
Christmas present in a few
days. It isn't dry yet. I
hope you like it! Love you.

M.

December 1

My dearest Mols,

I'm very sorry I haven't written or called
lately. I hope you haven't been worried. I
had a slight bug, and was out of commis-
sion for a while. I thought I had asked my
assistant to write to you, but she says I

didn't, so maybe I just thought I had.

Anyway, I'm feeling much better now. You would hardly recognize me! I've lost a lot of weight. Also, shaving is a pain in the jungle, so I've been growing in my beard. Tom (Tom Martkinson, from the studio) says it makes me look like a Viking. I'll try to send you a picture.

I just got your letter from Thanksgiving—I'm glad you have a new friend. I missed you a lot on Thanksgiving, but I was pretty sick, and it was hard for me to think about anything but getting better.

Today I'm mailing some instructions to Ms. Thacker about your birthday and Christmas presents. I want her to make your birthday really special. I can't believe it's only three weeks away. You'll be so old—eleven. I'm very proud of you, sweetie. You've been so brave and cheerful in your letters. It's been a big help.

This movie has been much more difficult than I figured on—but I still think I can wrap things up by late June, and then come home to you, Mols. I want you to start thinking about where we should go when I get back—we'll go anywhere you want. I'm just looking forward to a nice long rest, wherever it is.

Now I'd better go, honey. The first team is

ready for me. I can't wait to show this movie to you—we're getting some great stuff. I believe in it more than ever.

Take care, sweetie. Remember that your old dad loves you very much, all the time.

Love,
Dad

Molly set her father's letter down and wiped the tears from her cheeks. Outside, it was a cold December night, and snow was falling again in silent drifts. He had been sick! So sick that he couldn't write her for weeks. She tried to picture him with a beard, and all skinny from being ill. It almost broke her heart.

Mr. Tibbs, who was getting bigger every day, leaped up on the bed and began to settle down right on her father's letter. Molly snatched it up. Looking offended, Mr. Tibbs moved over a little bit, then started washing his hind leg.

Dad, I'm trying to be brave, but it's getting harder, not easier. I can't stand knowing that you were sick and I couldn't help you. The worst part was feeling so helpless. If she had been there, she could have taken care of him. But she hadn't even known about it.

She was stuck at Glenmore. She knew that. Her job was to stay there, be brave, and help her father from there in Boston any way she could. She decided that she would try to send him a little package—of vitamins, maybe, and cold medicine. Stuff that maybe he couldn't get very easily, but she could just buy at the pharmacy. It would probably take a long time to get to him, but it might help him when it finally arrived. And she would write a cheerful, funny letter, too, to cheer him up.

It was all she could do from so far away. Molly took out her notebook and began to make a list.

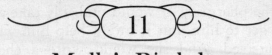

11

Molly's Birthday

"How do you think you did?" Molly asked Evie after their English final in mid-December.

Evie shrugged. "I think I did okay. I studied a lot, and English is pretty easy for me. It's the science that's gonna be a killer."

"Yeah." Molly nodded. "Me too. Let's get together and study for it."

"Me too," Lucy said, following them. "I'm totally lame in science. You guys can study sixth-grade stuff and I'll study seventh-grade stuff."

"Deal. I gotta go. Work-study. Later, guys." With a last wave, Evie left Molly and Lucy in the hall and headed off to Ms. Thacker's office.

"Every time I think about Evie's work-study program, I want to scream," Molly said angrily.

"I know what you mean," Lucy agreed.

As part of the charity-pupil deal, Evie was supposed to work at Glenmore for about eight hours a week. The people who had organized the program thought it would be a good way for their students to learn useful office skills, such as answering the phone, using a computer, filing, or whatever. It would help them get jobs later, when they were out of school.

But what they didn't know, Molly fumed as she and Lucy headed to their study hall, was that at Glenmore, Ms. Thacker's assistant did all the office work.

"It's like Evie's a slave or something," Lucy whispered as they took their seats in the junior lounge used for study halls.

"I know. It totally stinks," Molly whispered back.

Since Susan did all the office work, Ms. Thacker had Evie do other kinds of work—such as polishing the brass doorknobs, sweeping the long stairs, dusting the library, and washing windows. It made Molly furious. Once she had complained to Evie about it, and urged her to report the situation to the board of trustees, or whoever had put her there in the first place. But Evie had said no.

"Number one, what if they yanked me out of here and put me in another school where I *did* do office work? What if the new place wasn't as cool as Glenmore? What if the kids there totally hated me, and I didn't have even one friend?" Evie had argued. "Number two, I don't really mind doing that stuff. It isn't so bad. And it makes me feel like I'm earning my way, at least a little."

"But still," Molly persisted. "They have maids to do that stuff—maids who get paid. It isn't fair that they make you do all the worst stuff."

"Molly, look, just leave it," Evie said. "It's okay. Don't make trouble."

December 18

Dear Journal,
   Sorry I haven't written in a while. Now that I hang out with Lucy and Evie and Shannon, it seems like I'm always busy.
   Right now I'm sitting in my window seat. I can see almost all of Fitzgerald Square from here, and I love watching all the people. There's the old woman from the townhouse next to Glenmore who walks with her housekeeper, an old man who sits on a bench in the sun whenever it isn't absolutely freezing, a young couple with a big dog. . . . I love making up stories about

108

the people I see. I imagine
what their jobs are, and if
they have families, and what
they do for fun.

Maybe it's just because of
my birthday coming up, and
because Dad and I have never
been apart for it, but I've
been feeling really down lately,
and not even Lucy or Evie
can cheer me up. Shannon is
being so weird, she's no
help at all. It's like she's
ashamed of me and Lucy now
as well as Evie. She's started
eating lunch with Rebecca
Hirschman sometimes. I mean,
it's okay if she wants to be
friends with Rebecca, but the
whole thing just seems silly
to me.

Molly stopped writing for a moment and looked
out her window. The bare trees and wintry sky made
her feel lonely. With a sigh, she picked up her journal again.

Ms. Thacker gives me the creeps more and more. I see her talking to parents and she's so nice and smiley, kissing up to them and all. But then I see how she treats Evie and it makes me want to call a newspaper and have an exposé done on her. Or maybe I could write it myself. It would be my first investigative article.

I'd better go. I have one more final tomorrow, in math, and then we have the Christmas party, and vacation starts the afternoon of my birthday-December 22nd. I can't believe that Dad won't be here.

"Well, dahling, how do I look?" Evie slowly pirouetted in front of Molly. She was wearing her blue blazer and her gray pleated skirt.

"You look great. Very preppy," Molly said with a grin.

Evie shrugged. "They're the nicest clothes I have," she said matter-of-factly. Then she put on a fake-sounding voice. "And we all have to look our *best* for Miss Molly's famous birthday," she said with a simpering smile.

Laughing, Molly threw a sweat sock at her.

"Oh, please. Ms. Thacker's being silly about this whole thing," Molly said. "I mean, I know my dad wanted me to have a special birthday, but this whole elaborate party thing is just making me nervous."

"Now, dear," Evie whined, "you know we all just want our Mollykins to be happy. So put on your party duds and a great big Glenmore smile and come welcome all your little guests."

Molly tried to give a sarcastic groan, but began choking when it turned into a laugh. Finally she fell over on her side on the floor, giggling nervously.

"Well! Looks like you've got everything under control," Evie said brightly. "I'll see you downstairs, princess."

Molly grinned and waved. Then with a sigh she got up and started looking for something to wear. She meant what she'd told Evie—she thought Ms. Thacker was making too big a deal of her birthday. Her father had asked Ms. Thacker to, and Molly knew he meant well, but the huge party the headmistress had planned probably would just make the other students resent Molly.

"Thank heavens Lucy and Evie know better,"

111

Molly muttered as she found a dress that didn't need ironing.

Before she went downstairs, she read her father's latest letter one more time.

December 14 Via Airmail

Dearest Mols,

I'm very tired right now, but I've had a great day, and didn't want to go to sleep without writing to you, my own darling daughter. Today I showed a preliminary rough cut of about half the movie to a studio honcho, and he really loved it. He said it was great, destined for awards, an Oscar, etc. He may have just been sucking up, but he sounded sincere. We'll see. Anyway, it made me feel a lot better.

Do you remember me talking about my old friend, the one who was my teacher at film school? She did the film editing on *My Ruined Life*, back when you were just a baby. Anyway, we've kept in touch through the years, and she just sent me a telegram saying she will edit this movie. I'm really excited about it. She's one of the best in the business, and she doesn't accept too many jobs. Anyway, she's on her way here now. I warned her to expect primitive conditions.

So everything is falling into place, sweetie. Most of the principal shooting has been done, and we're just going in for the close-ups and some fill-in shots. Right now it looks like we might wrap it up on time!

Anyway, I'm feeling enthusiastic for the first time in months. The only thing that would make me happier is if you were here, too, or if I were there.

But enough about all my stuff. Have an absolutely wonderful birthday, and know that I am thinking about you every minute. I'll write again in a few days to see how your Christmas went. I'm glad Evie will be staying with you during the holidays.

> Lots of love and hugs and
> kisses from your old dad.
> XXOO

When at last Molly went downstairs, she found Ms. Thacker waiting for her.

"Happy birthday, Molly," she said, giving Molly a pretty smile. She was wearing a bright-red skirt and a red and green plaid sweater. She always wore neat clothes. "Everyone's waiting for you in the junior lounge. And then Mr. Bloch has prepared a special birthday lunch for all of us."

Molly smiled, but she wasn't sure if it came out as a smile or a grimace. She hated to be the center of attention—and now, on her birthday, she would be the center of attention all day long. Fortunately, a lot of kids had left early for the Christmas holidays, so only about sixty people were left. If it had really been everyone, Molly might have refused to come at all.

With another little sigh, she entered the junior lounge.

Inside, the lounge was all dressed up. Crepe-paper streamers in Christmasy colors looped from the ceiling down to the walls, and there were helium balloons tied in big bunches. A large HAPPY BIRTHDAY banner was tacked to one wall.

Looking around at her schoolmates, Molly felt that she could read their expressions. Lucy and Evie were genuinely glad for her, although a hint of a smirk was playing around Evie's mouth. Shannon was looking happy and sitting next to Rebecca. A lot of the boys were cutting up and asking loudly for refreshments. Several of the older students—including Celeste and Laura—were looking conspicuously bored. But then, they often looked like that.

"Ah, here you are," Mr. Thacker said, coming forward to lead Molly to the seat of honor, a large, overstuffed armchair. "Now the party can begin." He gave her a faint smile.

It was a real, Hollywood-like party, Molly thought an hour later. Whenever she and her dad had been in California, she had always gotten invited to parties of kids she barely knew. The only reason she used to go was so she could describe to her dad how outrageously extravagant they were.

One party had featured a whole team of synchronized swimmers spelling out *Happy Birthday* in the enormous swimming pool. And of course there were always ponies and clowns and stand-up comics. And the kids whose parents were stars always had their parents get copies of movies that hadn't officially been released yet.

This party at Glenmore seemed a little bit like that, except without any stars. But there was a magician who did all sorts of neat tricks with cards and his hat and his magic wand. At one point he pulled a whole bouquet of real flowers from behind Molly's ear. He was a good magician, but still, Molly felt uncomfortable having everyone watch her reaction.

Then it was time for lunch, and ice cream and cake. Augustus Bloch had made all of Molly's favorites, and when the kitchen assistants entered the dining room, everyone gasped at the sight of the huge, three-tiered cake.

"It looks like a wedding cake," Lucy whispered in awe, examining the cascade of pink sugar roses that was draped from the top layer all the way down.

"All right, students," Ms. Thacker said, clapping her hands. "Let's all remember our holiday manners. After lunch, Molly will begin cutting her cake."

Molly was just beginning to eat her cheeseburger when she saw Mr. Thacker come into the dining room looking nervous and upset. He whispered into his wife's ear. It was interesting to watch Ms. Thacker's expression of concern and irritation, quickly covered up with a fake smile. Then the headmistress got up and followed her husband out.

"Wonder what all that was about," Lucy said, helping herself to more fries.

Molly shrugged. "School business, I guess. Or maybe a pipe broke or something. Could you please pass the ketchup?"

12

There Must Be Some Mistake

It *was* school business of a sort that took Ms. Thacker out of the dining room in the middle of Molly's birthday lunch. Her husband had come in to tell her that one of Mr. Stewart's lawyers was waiting in her office. It was about Molly, and to Ms. Thacker, Molly was school business.

Now Ms. Thacker stood in her own private office. Although she wasn't tall, she had piercing black eyes and could look very intimidating when she needed to.

"Yes? I am the headmistress of the school," she said.

A sleek young man with smooth cheeks, wearing an expensive-looking suit, turned around. He didn't smile.

"Ms. Thacker, I'm Christopher Grassi from Morgenstein, Ehrenhaft, and Grassi. We represent, or rather represented, the late Michael Stewart."

For almost a minute Ms. Thacker was convinced

117

she hadn't heard him correctly. The *late* Michael Stewart? There had to be some mistake.

Finally she said, almost stammering, "What do you mean? What are you talking about?" Feeling as though her head were spinning, she sat down abruptly in her desk chair. She simply didn't understand what he was telling her, and when she didn't understand something, it made her angry. She felt angry now.

"I mean, Ms. Thacker," the young lawyer continued, "that, unfortunately, Michael Stewart died five days ago of cholera in the jungles of Brazil."

Dead! The rich father of her richest student! It was almost beyond imagining. In a split second Ms. Thacker thought of the generous checks Michael Stewart had sent to the school—some specified for Molly's use, some gratifyingly marked "for general school use." His money had paid for new landscaping in the garden, the expensive office chair in which Ms. Thacker now sat, new appliances in the kitchen . . . and now he was dead. With an indrawn breath Ms. Thacker tried to remember when the last check had come in. A month earlier.

With a great effort, she found her voice. "His estate?" Surely he had made some provisions.

"There is no estate," the lawyer said baldly. "Against our advice, he always laughed at the idea of making a will, or of providing for Molly's care if something should happen to him."

"Her relatives?" Ms. Thacker asked, feeling almost

faint. Her husband came to stand in back of her chair, his hand on her shoulder. Irritated, she brushed his hand away.

"There aren't any that we know of," said Mr. Grassi.

"What happens now?" Ms. Thacker cried. "A guardian will be appointed, surely, to manage Molly's inheritance—"

"I've been telling you," Mr. Grassi said, sounding impatient. "There is no inheritance. Over the last five months Mr. Stewart sank literally everything he had into this project. One of his major financial backers pulled out, and Mr. Stewart liquidated his assets in order to continue making his film. In fact, he died without paying our firm's last bill. He owed us a considerable sum of money."

Ms. Thacker felt as if she might scream. In the month since she had received Michael Stewart's last check, she had spent a great deal of the school's money on Molly. She had paid for the party going on across the hall, as well as all the presents. Beautiful, expensive presents. Presents too good for any child, much less the spoiled daughter of a tacky movie producer. Not to mention the stable bills for Molly's stupid pony, not to mention her wretched cat's vet bills! Just two weeks earlier the animal had swallowed a length of string and had been X-rayed. The bill had been huge. Huge!

"What are my options?" Ms. Thacker said coldly,

119

trying desperately to rein in her emotions. "Is there no one I can sue to recover my losses?"

Mr. Grassi looked irritated. "No one. I assure you that if there were, we would have gotten to them first."

"And what of—the girl?" Ms. Thacker couldn't bring herself to say Molly's name. "Does she go to an orphanage? A state home? Foster care?"

The lawyer shrugged. "No doubt a social worker will be able to advise you on that. I'm only here to tell you that she isn't our responsibility, and that she has no legal guardian."

"Well, she isn't *my* responsibility, I know that much," Ms. Thacker snapped. Without any money, Molly was useless to her. There was no way Ms. Thacker would put up with the girl's obnoxious, quiet superiority if it wasn't going to be worth her while. "I'm calling social services right now. They can come get her today."

The lawyer looked at her with ill-disguised contempt. "It's your decision, unfortunately," he said, standing up to leave. "I feel sorry for the child. Her father was all she had in the world—and now she has no one."

Ms. Thacker tightened her lips but made no reply as the lawyer left.

As soon as the lawyer was gone Ms. Thacker exploded. "I can't believe the man! His carelessness! He goes and gets himself killed in some ridiculous jungle, and he doesn't even have a will!"

"Dear, please lower your voice," Mr. Thacker said urgently. "I know you're upset—it's a terrible thing."

"Terrible?" Ms. Thacker stared at her husband with wide eyes. "Do you know how much I spent on that party across the hall? Do you know what I spent on presents?"

Mr. Thacker shrugged his shoulders, looking helpless. "Yes, it's awful, but what can we do? You heard Mr. Grassi. There's nothing and no one we can turn to."

Ms. Thacker sat down and put her head in her hands. "I don't believe this is happening," she said bitterly. "Molly Stewart was exactly the kind of student this dump needed—tons of money and a father who spoiled her rotten. Now she's just a millstone."

"The poor thing is going to be very upset," Mr. Thacker said, pacing nervously. "Her father was all she had. I don't envy her. Should I call the social worker?"

"No," Ms. Thacker snapped. "I need time to think. I don't know what we're going to do. In the meantime, send her in to me. Break up that ridiculous party, and box up the presents so they can be returned."

"Oh, dear, are you sure—" Mr. Thacker began.

Ms. Thacker gave him a piercing glare.

"I'll go get her," he said, and left the room quickly.

*   *   *

Molly had no idea what Ms. Thacker wanted, right in the middle of the party. But she put down the last present she had opened up, a huge, beautiful book on horses, and followed Mr. Thacker to the office.

When Molly went in, Ms. Thacker was pacing in front of the fireplace at the end of the office. She looked mad about something.

"Mr. Thacker said you wanted to see me?"

"Molly, I have bad news," Ms. Thacker said abruptly.

Molly's first thought was, *Mr. Tibbs?*

"Your father's lawyer just came to see us. He told us that your father died of cholera five days ago, in Brazil."

Molly stared at Ms. Thacker. Could the headmistress really be so mean as to play such a sick joke? But Ms. Thacker's dark eyes were boring into her own wide green ones, and a tiny portion of her brain registered the awful truth. *It's not a joke.*

"What do you mean?" Molly didn't recognize the fragile, trembling voice as her own.

"Your father died, Molly, five days ago," Ms. Thacker snapped. "Even worse, there's no money. Nothing. Nothing!" Ms. Thacker looked enraged, and she threw up her arms and paced again on the Oriental rug.

"I don't . . . I don't . . ." Molly felt that she was looking through a long dark tunnel, and the only thing she could see was Ms. Thacker's face, glowing whitely with two black coals for eyes, at the other end.

"It's really very simple, Molly," Ms. Thacker said, looking at her as if she hated her. "You have no money. Apparently you have no relatives, either."

"What—what will . . ." Molly was having a very hard time forming the words. She didn't even know what she wanted to say. It was all too much for her to take in.

"I don't know what will happen to you," Ms. Thacker said, turning her back on Molly. "We have very few options. Go up to your room now and let me think. I can't talk to you anymore."

Wordlessly, feeling as though she were anesthetized, Molly stumbled out of Ms. Thacker's office and into the hall. Several students were milling around, gazing at her curiously, but Molly ignored them.

Then Lucy and Evie stepped forward, one on each side, and with them as her guards Molly walked like a sleepwalker down the hall. Upstairs, in front of her room, Lucy squeezed her hand.

"I'll come in with you," she whispered. Molly didn't know why she was whispering.

"Me too," Evie said, her voice thick.

"No. No, thank you," Molly said. Her voice sounded distant to her own ears.

"Molly, talk to us," Evie urged. "Mr. Thacker wouldn't tell us what happened."

"I can't talk," Molly mumbled. "I think I'll just be alone for a while."

123

Even as she was turning the cold brass knob and letting herself into her room, the thought came to her. *For the rest of my life.* Then she shut the door right in the faces of her two best friends.

An hour later, sitting in her room, holding Mr. Tibbs to her chest, Molly felt as if the news still hadn't sunk in. She tried repeating it to herself again and again, as though somehow the words would imprint themselves on her brain in a way that she could understand.

"Dad is dead," she murmured into Mr. Tibbs's soft gray fur. "My father is dead. Dad is dead. He's never coming back. Not ever. I'll never see him again." Reaching beneath her shirt, she felt for the gold heart locket that he had given her just three and a half months before. Her fingers traced the delicate engraving. Since he had left, she had worn it always. She would continue to wear it, always.

A fierce pain consumed her; it seemed to be eating at her insides. She was in too much pain to cry. Some part of her realized that later there would be tears, awful, wracking, choking sobs, but just then she was in shock, and her eyes were dry.

"Dad is dead," she mumbled. "My dad is dead. I'm alone."

She sat like that for quite some time, until the afternoon sun slanted deeply into her windows, tinting the walls a golden orange. It was her eleventh birthday, and her father was dead, and they would never be together again.

When Molly entered Ms. Thacker's office the next day, her face was pinched and white, her green eyes huge and haunted. Her long blond hair was hanging down limply, and she was wearing a plain sweatshirt and some leggings. She noticed that for the first time the headmistress didn't bother to plaster a smile on her face.

"Molly, the news about your father has had serious consequences for everyone," Ms. Thacker began in a cool voice. "Of course you are the most affected, but Glenmore, and myself personally, are paying a high price for the foolishness of trusting your father to honor his debts."

What are you getting at, you witch? Suddenly hating Ms. Thacker, Molly stood before her, very still, biting her lip and yet trying to appear as if she didn't want to run screaming from the room.

"In short, Molly, you are an orphan," Ms. Thacker said cruelly. "You have no money; your father's fortune is gone. His unfinished film is worth nothing. His production company will be broken up and sold to pay his creditors, of whom there are many. And you are left without a home, without a legal guardian."

Molly was silent. She knew all this, but it was hard to understand why any of it mattered now, why anything mattered at all when her father was dead.

"You have two options, Molly," Ms. Thacker continued. "One option is to go into foster care. A social worker will come, and eventually a place will be found for you with some family. I don't know where."

Molly had heard Evie talk about foster homes. They sounded pretty bad. On the other hand, nothing could really be worse than knowing she would never see her father again. *There isn't much that can get to me now,* Molly thought numbly. *Not even Ms. Thacker.*

"The other option," the headmistress continued, "is to remain here at Glenmore."

Molly's eyes widened. How would that be possible? There was no money. That was what everyone kept telling her. There was no money.

"You could remain here as a charity pupil, like Eve Lucas," Ms. Thacker explained stiffly. "I would be appointed your legal guardian. You would move up to the fifth floor, with the servants. Your expensive clothes, toys, TV, all that nonsense, would be bundled up and either sold or given to a tax-deductible charity so that I can begin to make up my extensive losses. You would also have certain responsibilities around here, just as Eve does. I would consider your work an opportunity for you to pay me back for the large sums of money that I'll never recover from your father's estate. In return, you will have room and board, and your education—an education, I remind you, that costs other children a

126

great deal. You may have one hour to decide. You are dismissed."

Without a word, Molly turned and left Ms. Thacker's office. It was lunchtime, and as Molly hadn't eaten dinner the night before or breakfast that morning, she was aware of an empty, gnawing feeling inside. But going to the dining room would mean facing everyone, and Molly was sure they all knew about her father by now.

Then Lucy came running down the main staircase, checking her watch as if worried that she was late for lunch. When she saw Molly standing there indecisively, her face lit up, then immediately sobered.

"Oh, Mol," she said breathlessly.

Molly just looked at Lucy silently. What could she say?

"Molly, I was so worried about you last night. Is there anything I can do? What's going to happen to you now? Is someone going to come get you?"

It felt as if a heavy weight were pressing on Molly's chest, and she couldn't answer.

Lucy took one look at Molly's face. Then, holding Molly by the hand, she pulled her gently toward the dining room door. "Come on," she said briskly. "You need something to eat. You can sit right by me and Evie. We won't let anyone bug you."

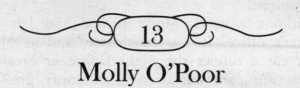

13

Molly O'Poor

For Molly the next week passed in a blur. Lucy was forced to go home for Christmas vacation, but called every day. Christmas Day had no meaning for Molly, though Evie gave her a book she had wanted, and she mindlessly gave Evie the new sweater she'd bought her two weeks before.

Molly had decided to stay at Glenmore, partly to be with her friends and partly because she still had one tiny, flickering hope that somehow, somewhere, she belonged to someone. Maybe there was even a chance that her father wasn't really dead—that it was all just a horrible mistake. In that case, Molly wanted to be sure to stay in the same place he had left her.

The social worker came and explained everything to her, but Molly barely understood anything. She signed her name again and again to papers saying that she was choosing to stay at Glenmore, and that she understood that Mr. and Ms. Thacker were her legal guardians. As soon as the papers were signed and the social worker was gone, Ms. Thacker told Molly to go to her room and pack up everything to be given away.

Inside the comfortable, pleasant room she had lived in for the past three and a half months, Molly looked around. She would miss her window seats, miss people-watching out the windows. With a wry grin she realized she would miss having her own bathroom. On the fifth floor, she would have to share with Evie and the female live-in help.

Mr. Tibbs, as if sensing her jumbled emotions, came to step daintily across her lap, swishing his fat, fluffy tail against her neck. She smoothed his fur and kissed his head. He purred and bumped his head against her chest.

Then Molly began to pack. As she loaded her computer and all her software into a cardboard box she thought of the conversation she had had with Lucy and Evie. Evie had told her definitely *not* to go into foster care.

"You don't want to do that, trust me," she had said. "You have no idea where you'll end up. I'm sure there are some nice families out there, but who knows if you'll get one? You might be assigned to a family where the parents are awful and mean, and the kids hate you. No, you'd better stay here, no matter what."

"I can't believe Ms. Thacker offered to let you stay. I thought she was meaner than that. Maybe she really cares about you," Lucy had said.

Evie had snorted. "Yeah, like a snake cares about a mouse," she had said roughly. "Don't you know that she gets money for her charity students?"

"She does?"

"Of course she does! She gets a tax break for scholarship kids, like Shannon, but she gets actual money from the government for charity kids, like me. It doesn't cost her anything to keep me—she probably *makes* money."

"Gee, I didn't know that," Lucy had said.

"No reason why you should," Molly had said.

That conversation had taken place before Lucy had gone home for Christmas. But, Molly thought as she made a stack of her cashmere sweaters and dropped them in a box, it hadn't changed her mind. She still wanted to be where her father last left her. She didn't know how long Ms. Thacker would let her stay at Glenmore—maybe only as long as she made herself useful. But she couldn't really think about the future right then. She would have to take things one day at a time.

Ms. Thacker strode into the room. She no longer had to knock. "Keep some serviceable clothes," she instructed, "but you won't need any of your extravagant designer outfits anymore."

"I'm already packing them," Molly answered evenly.

"Where's the animal's carry case?"

Frowning, Molly asked, "What for?"

"I won't pay another cent to keep that flea-bitten

parasite in this house any longer," Ms. Thacker said coldly, glaring at Mr. Tibbs, who was on the window seat. His round copper-colored eyes glared back at her. "I feel ill when I think of what I've paid in vet bills alone! Give him to me. He's going to the pound."

"No!" Molly cried, horrified at the thought of her sweet Mr. Tibbs sitting in some crowded wire cage at the pound.

"He isn't staying. It was foolish of me to allow you to keep him—I certainly won't let another student take him."

"No, I mean you don't have to take him to the pound. I—I'll take him," Molly stammered.

Ms. Thacker hesitated, looking at Molly with narrowed eyes. "Don't you try to hide him," she said sternly. "I don't want him in this dorm."

"I won't. I'll take him away," Molly said. Nervously her finger tapped against her locket.

"I'll need that locket, please, along with your other jewelry," Ms. Thacker said, holding out her hand. "Your father was far too generous with you, but perhaps I can sell the items to recoup some of your expenses."

Wordlessly Molly rose and crossed the room to her dresser. She picked up her velvet-lined jewelry box and practically flung it at Ms. Thacker. It contained small diamond studs, her birthstone ring, several gold chains, other gold earrings, and a strand of real pearls that she had gotten for her tenth birthday.

"Here," she said, trying to control the anger in

her voice. "Take them, all of them. But you can't have the locket—ever."

An angry flush mottled Ms. Thacker's face. "You don't seem to appreciate your position here," she said in a harsh, mean voice. "If it weren't for me, you'd be out on the street. And you show your gratitude by withholding a piece of ridiculous jewelry? Give it to me at once."

Molly's jaw was set and her eyes flashed. Suddenly she felt tall and fierce, and far, far older than her eleven years. "If you want this locket," she said in a low, serious voice, "you will have to kill me first." Her eyes bored into Ms. Thacker's like icy daggers.

"Very well," Ms. Thacker said abruptly, turning away. "Keep the tacky locket. I want you out of this room by five o'clock, and I want that animal gone in one hour. Do you understand?"

"I understand very well, Ms. Thacker," Molly replied in disgust.

After the headmistress had swept out, Molly sank onto her bed. Somehow she had pictured having Mr. Tibbs in her new attic room, pictured coming home to him after a long, tiring, depressing day and having him comfort her. But she was not to have even that. Sighing, Molly tried to hold herself together. At least she had kept the locket.

Now she had to do the hardest thing she had ever done in her life. She fished Mr. Tibbs's wicker case out from the bottom of the closet. She put a towel in the bottom so he wouldn't hurt his feet, and wrapped another towel around the sides so he wouldn't freeze outside. She also put in some of his favorite toys and his purebred registration papers. She scratched out her name on the papers with a black pen. Then she tugged on a sweatshirt and grabbed her backpack.

Mr. Tibbs was still on the window seat, watching her carefully. Molly went to sit by him.

"Tibbsey," she said softly, stroking his fur, "you know I love you very, very much. Things have changed, though, and I can't keep you. But I'm going to find someone who will take good care of you and love you just as much as I do. Okay? We had some good times together, didn't we?" She buried her face in his fluffy side. "You know I'll always love you. And I'll miss you. But we have to go now."

Then she gently urged him into his carrier, grabbed her heavy coat, and walked downstairs, grateful that the school was pretty empty. She couldn't have faced anyone else at that moment. She didn't really know where she was going on that sunny, cold, clear winter day. In her mind she had a vague idea about offering Mr. Tibbs to a nice-looking stranger in the park. She knew taking him to the pound was out of the question.

At the end of the block she turned the corner, and at the end of that block she turned the corner again. She was walking past the high brick wall in back of Glenmore.

Glenmore took up almost the entire block. There was only one townhouse next to it, on the very end. Molly looked into its rear garden. She knew an elderly woman lived in that stone townhouse; sometimes Molly saw the woman's housekeeper accompanying her on a walk when the weather was nice.

Their yard was bordered by a black wrought-iron fence. There was a gate in the middle. The yard might have been beautiful once, but it was overgrown now with large bushes and trees and untrimmed hedges. As Molly was standing there the back door opened and a uniformed housekeeper, the one Molly had seen before, put out a milk bottle with a note in it. Molly shrank back out of sight until she heard the door close.

Then an idea came to her. *Old ladies = cats.* Was it possible that Mr. Tibbs could live right next door? The two women seemed like nice people. The elderly woman always smiled at other people and greeted them on her walks. And the housekeeper didn't look mean.

Molly made a quick decision. She would try these people first. If they opened the door and sounded disgusted or angry when they saw Mr. Tibbs, Molly could quickly run up and say it had all been a mistake.

Putting down the heavy wicker carrier, Molly took a piece of paper and a pen out of her backpack.

Mr. Tibbs mewed loudly and rattled the sides of his basket. Molly hoped he wasn't too cold. It was freezing out. Quickly Molly wrote a note and attached it to the basket's handle. It read: *My name is Mr. Tibbs. I am a purebred British Blue. I am very sweet and friendly and never scratch. My owner loves me but can't keep me anymore. Please take good care of me, or give me to a caring friend. Thank you.*

Then Molly crept up the brick walkway to the back door. Mr. Tibbs stuck his paw out of the basket, and Molly gently touched it. "I love you," she said, her voice cracking a tiny bit. "I'll always love you."

Then she put the basket down on the cold stone doorstep, rang the doorbell, and ran to hide in some nearby bushes.

The back door opened almost immediately.

"Who's there?" asked a pleasant voice. Then, "Oh, my! What's this?"

From where she was crouched beneath a huge rhododendron bush, Molly saw the housekeeper bend down to read the note on the basket. She heard Mr. Tibbs meow loudly. The maid tilted the basket and looked inside.

"Well, now, Mr. Tibbs, you sure are a pretty boy," the maid said. "I wonder who would give up such a pretty darling on such a cold day. Well, you just come inside and let's see if I have a little tuna fish for you. Maybe you can stay with us."

Then the door closed, and the maid was gone. So was Mr. Tibbs. And so was Molly's last connection to her father, besides her locket.

There, beneath the bushes of the house next door, Molly put her head in her hands and allowed herself to cry for the first time since she had found out her father was dead. She fell over onto the damp, cold, sweet-smelling earth and sobbed, finally letting out some measure of the unbearable pain and grief she had been overwhelmed with for the past week.

She didn't know how long she lay there, but finally her choking sobs subsided to dry, racking coughs, and minutes after that, she lay silent. After her face had dried and she had wiped her hands on her jeans, she sat up, feeling almost light-headed and foggy. Clumsily she brushed leaves and dirt out of her hair, and rubbed her face against her sleeve. When she stood up she felt shaky.

It was time to go back to Glenmore, to her new room. She could no longer think about Mr. Tibbs or about the way her life used to be. She was starting a new life, one she would have to accept for as long as she lived.

She'd better get to it.

Don't miss *A Room in the Attic*,
the next book in this
heartwarming new series.

"Maybe someday we can have our own bakery," Molly said, smiling at Evie. "We'll call it EM's. E for Evie, M for Molly. And we'll just bake pastries all day, and bread."

"And sticky buns," Evie agreed enthusiastically. "And muffins." She concentrated on squeezing the pastry bag, and made a nice, even ribbon around a heart-shaped cookie.

"That would be great," Molly said, picturing their little shop in her mind. Lucy could be in on it, too, and maybe Mr. Tibbs would be there, keeping mice away. It would be so fabulous. So different from Glenmore.

"Who dusted the library?"

Ms. Thacker's enraged voice snapped Molly's head around. The dreamy smile left her face.

"Is something wrong?" Molly asked.

"Yes!" Ms. Thacker hissed. "Was it you?"

"Um . . ." Molly began.

137

"No, it was me," Evie said, her dark eyebrows meeting in a frown. "Did I miss a section?"

"I'll tell you what you *didn't* miss," the headmistress snarled. Her face was white with anger, and her hands were actually trembling. For a moment Molly thought Ms. Thacker would hit Evie.

Evie looked at her, not comprehending.

The headmistress held out a large porcelain shard. Molly recognized it as part of one of the matching china urns on either side of the library fireplace. It looked as though one of them had been broken. Had Evie done it? Molly looked at her friend.

Instantly she knew that Evie was innocent. Molly remembered how Evie had looked when she came into the kitchen. She had been tired but relaxed. There was no guilt or worry on her face.

"Don't look at *me*," Evie said, her face setting in a scowl. "I didn't break that thing. When I left the library, it was standing there, the same as always."

"Then how do you explain this?" Ms. Thacker pushed the sharp shard close to Evie's face. Evie didn't flinch.

"Why don't you ask one of those boys who was playing paper football in there while I was dusting?" Evie said. "They were the ones horsing around. I'm always real careful." Her chin jutted out and she looked at Ms. Thacker defiantly.

The headmistress's dark eyes seemed to shoot sparks at Evie. "Don't lie to me," she said in a loud voice. "Don't try to blame your clumsiness on some

innocent *paying* students! I know you did this."
Again she shook the china shard in the air.

It was too much for Molly to bear. The entire
kitchen was quiet, and everyone was watching the
ugly scene. Molly could see the heat rise in Evie's face.

"Don't blame her!" Molly cried angrily, facing
Ms. Thacker. "She said she didn't do it, so she
didn't. Just because a kid's parents are paying tuition doesn't mean they're perfect and would never
break anything! That's crazy."

Ms. Thacker's eyes widened until Molly thought
they were going to pop out of her head. Her mouth
tightened into an angry slash, and the hand not
holding the shard was curled into a pink-tipped
claw. Molly wanted to take a step back, but refused
to give the headmistress the satisfaction.

"Shut up!" Ms. Thacker shrieked. "You can't say
anything! You're only here because I didn't want to
put you out into the street, you . . . you . . . *orphan*!"

Molly felt the blood drain out of her face.

Ms. Thacker turned to Evie again. "I know you did
this, and you're going to pay. Both of you. You're just
as much to blame as Eve is," she told Molly. "You're
both grounded until further notice. That means no
dance tonight, no visiting your friends, no privileges of
any kind. You'll take your meals here, in the kitchen.
When you're not in class or working, you'll be in your
rooms, alone. And I *will* be checking up on you."

139